*Fatal Observations*

*By the same author*

LEAVING THE LIGHT ON

# Fatal Observations

## CATHERINE MERRIMAN

VICTOR GOLLANCZ

LONDON

First published in Great Britain 1993
by Victor Gollancz
A Cassell imprint
Villiers House, 41/47 Strand, London WC2N 5JE

A catalogue record for this book is
available from the British Library.

ISBN 0 575 05376 3

Typeset at The Spartan Press Ltd,
Lymington, Hants
and printed in Great Britain by
St Edmundsbury Press Ltd,
Bury St Edmunds, Suffolk

*For Ray and Val*
*in whose flat, of course,*
*nothing like this happened*

# Prologue

Ruth always said Harry had a death wish. Not of the suicidal variety; she used to reckon he was definitely saving himself up for an obliging enemy to do the job for him. And although she laughed, it wasn't a joke. I don't believe in death wishes myself, not the kind Ruth means, but then she knew him a lot longer than I did, and her theory may give her comfort, so I wouldn't like to knock it.

He was different, I'll give her that. She once said he was the exact opposite of a bully, and though the description implied virtues he didn't deserve, I knew what she meant. Show him an irate old lady or a difficult child, or anyone who couldn't possibly be a threat to him, and his patience and tolerance were boundless. Show him someone who could actually do him harm – policemen, antagonistic men of any complexion, assuming they were large enough or in sufficient quantities to be taken seriously – and he rose to the occasion immediately. Which of course only made dangerous situations worse.

I think I know why he was like that, though I can't be sure. And I wouldn't tell Ruth even if I was, because she might think she was partly to blame, and that wouldn't be fair. In any case we've never talked much about his background, so it has to be mostly guesswork. But I know his mother died when he was in his early teens, which may have had something to do with it. And that for the rest of his adolescence he lived a nomadic existence with his father, a drill sergeant in the army, and reputedly a great believer in brave faces and standing on your own feet, which may have had something to do with it too. Apparently his father would have liked Harry to join him in the army, but even if Harry had wanted to I can't imagine it would have worked. By the time he'd reached the age for that sort of decision he must have made enough brave faces and stood on his own two feet at enough bases round the country to make him quite unsuitable for the disciplines of army life.

Ruth and I still talk about him, even now. It takes time, doesn't it, to see the whole story.

# Chapter 1

Harry and Ruth moved into the ground floor flat two floors below me, in the spring of 1984.

It's important I describe the flats: they were a purpose-built block of nine in Kilburn, North London. One of those red-brick thirties blocks, with two entrances, the main one serving six of the flats, three storeys high and mirror image to each other, and the other serving the remaining three, with me at the top.

The flat below mine, like the furthermost top flat in the main block, had been empty for some months. When the bottom flat too fell vacant we were surprised to hear they were re-letting it. We'd understood – or rather the rumour was – that the landlord was hoping eventually to sell, not rent, but was waiting for several to fall vacant before sprucing them up for a killing on the self-contained market.

So I'd been surprised by the news, but mostly relieved: I'd been dreading the prospect of being the only occupant on my side, and had had nightmares of queues of tramps sleeping in the lobby, inspired by finding one very pathetic individual, who nevertheless terrified me when I fell over him one evening, and who at the time I hadn't had the courage to throw out. Luckily he had vanished, never to return, by the morning. More realistically, I'd also thought that leaving the ground floor flat empty was an open invitation to squatters (an unoccupied flat looks it, however many lace curtains you hang in the windows) and whilst I was not opposed to squatters as a species – in many ways it is an enterprising act, to squat, and in some parts of London, at least in those days, it was considered respectable and even status-enhancing to say you lived in one – all the same, there are squats, and squats. Moreover, if that flat were squatted they would soon get to know about the other empty flats, and I could see myself ending up as the only legitimate tenant above a sea of God knows what. As a single woman living alone, which had a few background fears to it anyway, mixed in with the countless blessings, I felt I could do without that. I suspect similar fears had occurred to the agents, which explained why they were letting that flat and not the others, and it was a great weight off my mind.

I knew very little about Ruth and Harry before they moved in. I'd caught the agent's assistant checking the place out before it was handed over, and tried to pump him about the new tenants, but he was a surprisingly secretive young man; all I got was that it was a couple, and not an old couple, which I deduced from his 'at least it won't be exclusively a geriatric home'. Cheeky sod, I thought; I was only thirty-six myself at the time. There was, however, an element of truth in his remark. Most of the other flats – in fact all except the one occupied by Mrs Gardiner and her six-year-old daughter – were tenanted by people who if not technically geriatric could nevertheless be described as in their late middle ages or beyond, and old Mrs Bundy would have probably been insulted to hear herself so euphemistically rejuvenated.

So I discovered that the new tenants were a youngish couple – he didn't mention any children – and one of them was a solicitor, which surprised me somewhat, as I thought a solicitor could have done rather better than our flats. Still, I thought, perhaps he was only recently qualified.

(I was misled into assuming it was the man. I should have known better, but it is easy to swallow half-buried allusions uncritically when one is basking in self-congratulation at having spotted them at all.)

Their removal van – self-hire with a Brighton address and telephone number painted in enormous white characters on the side – arrived on a Saturday morning, about a week after my encounter with the agent's assistant. I had a ringside view from my sitting room window, which overlooked the road below. You weren't meant to park outside the flats, but obviously it had to, half on and half off the pavement, and I took my toast and marmalade from a late breakfast over to the window and propped myself against the back of the settee to watch.

Three people got out of the van, two men and a woman. I automatically studied the woman first, I'm not sure why; perhaps because I expected or hoped to become neighbourly, and wanted to assess her as a potential friend. Or perhaps because I could be reasonably confident that she was one of the tenants, and it would have been a waste of effort to start on the men, when either or both might have turned out to be borrowed muscle for the move.

She was younger than me, I thought, but not much younger. Around thirty. Wearing jeans and sweater, but still managing to look remarkably neat and well groomed. Some people have an enviable physical integrity that allows them to look presentable in just about anything, and she struck me immediately as one of those. She had light brown hair, shoulder-length and curly – much the style I fancied trying myself, when I finally grew out of long hair – and she wore glasses with stylish red frames that matched her sweater. She wasn't pretty, but not plain either; more competent and vivacious-looking. Highly promising anyway, I thought.

Then I turned my attention to the men, who by now had started humping furniture off the van. It seemed self-evident straight away which was her partner. He had the same essentially neat style, and although he was in fact wearing cords and a stripy sweater with holes in the elbows, he came across as someone who didn't normally look like that, someone dressing down for the menial job in hand. He was tall, fairish like her, with an impeccably respectable beard, and I could see him as a solicitor. In any case, it had to be him, because – moving my gaze along – it couldn't be the other. This one was slightly shorter, though still a good five ten or so, and looked exactly like well-chosen muscle for the job. It was only early May, with a definite bite in the air, but within minutes he had stripped off his leather jacket (bomber style, unstudded, but still suspiciously like a motorbike jacket) to bare arms and a black sleeveless T-shirt. He was darker than the other two, with mid-brown close-cropped hair, and clean shaven, but it was difficult to see his face properly because he had a slouching style that meant he was permanently staring at the ground, an attitude he somehow managed to maintain even when he was actually carrying something. So I had an excellent view of the top of his head (and some impressive biceps) but not much else. I did however assume he was younger than the others, though why, on such scant evidence, I'm not sure. Something to do with the slouch, perhaps, something adolescent in it.

Having spied out the land, as it were, I was about to do my neighbourly duty and offer cups of tea when I saw myself beaten to it by Mrs Rosen, from the ground floor flat adjacent to theirs, who came tripping out of the main entrance with a laden tray, face wreathed in nosy welcome. The two men were carrying a divan bed from the van at the time, and they dumped it temporarily on the tiny strip of green behind the low perimeter wall to accept their cups. Mrs Rosen stayed chatting to them for a few minutes, and then with an undulating wave of her arm (which was presumably to indicate from which flat she had emerged but from my vantage point looked momentarily as if she was about to break into an Indian snake dance) left them drinking.

As she disappeared I saw the woman turn smiling to the fair-haired man, and he laughed in response. It was difficult not to laugh at Mrs Rosen on first meeting, and I certainly had, but I didn't any more. She and her husband had been there longest of all the tenants, and didn't like you to forget it. They owned it all. I'd been in the flat six years, that spring, and they still occasionally asked me how I was settling in. He looked like a gnome: tiny, chubby, and almost completely bald, and she like a much bigger person who had mysteriously shrunk, perhaps to accommodate herself to her husband's diminutive size, so that flaps and folds hung all over her. I'd like to be able to say that what she lacked in appeal physically she made up for in character, but I'm afraid even that wasn't true. I've never met anyone with such an insatiable appetite for bad news; if she couldn't get it she simply made it up. I shuddered to think what she said about me behind my back, because I was sure she was intelligent under that falsely innocent exterior, and undoubtedly knew I disliked her. We used to have the most ridiculous needling conversations that made me feel ashamed afterwards, as if I'd demeaned myself by stooping to her level. We'd part with viciously insincere smiles, her to enumerate my immoral vices to anyone who would listen – I could just imagine how 'And that nice young man who was here last weekend, such a good-looking boy' got translated out of my hearing – and me to spit venom in the kitchen and swear I'd give the old bag the taste of a few home truths one of these days.

But anyhow, after I'd been to the kitchen to dunk my coffee mug and plate in the bowl I returned to the window, in time to witness a scene that showed just how wrong hasty assumptions can be. The tall fair man strolled round to the main entrance with the empty cups, and while the others waited for him – nothing else could be unpacked while the path was blocked – the woman sat down on the abandoned divan. The darker young man sat down next to her and then did something quite unexpected. Admittedly they can't have known they were overlooked, and they would have been hidden from the traffic by the van and the garden wall, but the action was still surprising. He put a hand on her breast, pushed her backwards across the bed, and kissed her, sliding a leg over her thigh as he did it, so that for a moment he was lying half across her. The embrace lasted only a second or so before she twisted away and sat up laughing, but the act had been so intimate and familiar that it left no doubt in my mind as to whose partner she was.

Oh Christ, I thought, and pulled back immediately. I was half afraid the woman lying on her back for those few seconds had seen me, but mostly I was dismayed that it was he who was going to be my new neighbour, and not the fair man, whom I had already decided looked approachable and friendly. This one didn't; in fact although I had now seen his face, tilted upwards as he gave the woman a knowing, mock-hungry grin – practically a leer – the sight in no way contradicted the loutish first impression. I was astonished. True, he no longer looked so young – mid-twenties, at a guess – but he still didn't go with her at all, and the other had been a natural for the part.

★

14

I discovered later that the fair man was Ruth's brother. I should have guessed; they are very alike, give or take a beard. No wonder they made a couple.

And Ruth and Harry just did not go together. I couldn't make them out at all at first. All my neighbourly advances went by the board. I did nip down over that moving-in weekend to introduce myself, naturally, but they were busy and I had called at an inconvenient time, or at least I was left with that impression (of course I didn't know how Harry operated in those days). So the exchanges were brief, and didn't consist of much more on my part than 'Hello, I'm Jane Hardy, from upstairs,' and an offer to lend them anything they couldn't lay their hands on while they were living out of packing cases, but they didn't take me up on it, so they were either extremely well organized, or they didn't want to.

And after that it was difficult to make contact. For once I wished I was part of a couple, just for this one purpose; it makes things so much easier. If I'd been a couple I could have wandered down in the evening and suggested they join both of me in the pub for a chat, but as me on my own it would have lacked conviction. The pubs round there weren't the kind I'd have considered going to alone, not because I'd have feared for my reputation or my virtue, but because they were all boring drinking-men's preserves with nothing except some fancy Victorian mirrorwork to recommend them, and were only really tolerable for a quick one in the company of friends, when surroundings are unimportant. And somehow I felt awkward about calling down in the evening without an excuse when there was only me on my side, and two of them on theirs, and one of them was him.

The daytime was out, too. I was home for periods during the day; I lectured at a college of further education (Communication Skills – ha! – and Liberal Studies) and because I worked two evenings I had two free afternoons and one late morning, plus long holidays. But Ruth was out all day, either at the Law Centre in Camden or at her practice in Belsize Park, so if anyone was around in the daytime it was him, and I didn't feel I could pop down for a cup of coffee like I might have with a woman, even if I had wanted to, which at that stage I have to admit I didn't, greatly.

We did of course occasionally bump into each other. I would give him a bright, 'Hello!' (I know it sounds bright because people are always demanding to know what I've got to be so cheerful about) and he would grunt something incomprehensible in reply, and that would be that. Our meetings, brief though they were, always managed to make me feel silly, and somehow reduced. It was his closed-up expression: it made me feel that while he had the privilege of inspecting me, the same was not true in reverse, because he was hiding safely behind his inscrutability. Most frustrating too, because I knew that when he let the guard down he was capable of a charming smile. I received it one evening, inadvertently, when I was returning from work. As I passed their door he flung it wide – obviously mistaking me for Ruth – and for a moment I had a glimpse of a quite different Harry, relaxed and almost affectionate, before the shutters came down and he muttered, 'Oh it's you,' in a rudely disappointed tone, leaving me to stomp irritably up the stairs grumbling, 'Yes, only poor old boring me' to the worn-out lino.

It sounds silly to say I was offended by such unneighbourliness, especially as I had already decided that he probably wasn't worth getting to know, but I was. After all, I told myself, he couldn't possibly know what I thought of him, and I didn't see why if I was prepared to make the effort, feeling as I did, he shouldn't have the grace to meet me halfway. To be left high and dry in those circumstances is particularly galling.

I also couldn't think what he was doing around the place all day. To begin with it was understandable, because he was manifestly devoting time and energy to the flat. I could hear the whine of drills meeting brickwork, and once or twice I saw him sauntering home carrying timber and cans of paint. But that lasted only a month or so, and afterwards he was still around most of the day. I could tell because he played very loud rock music. Not that I objected; I listened to rock myself, and in any case it is one of the virtues of those solid thirties flats that sound doesn't travel very far. I could hear it when I passed their front door, but hardly at all from upstairs, even with the echo-chamber of an empty flat between. Still, I did wonder why he wasn't out at work, or tramping the streets looking for it, like everybody else.

Then, in the last week of June, his motorbike arrived. Delivered on a trailer, a vast and ancient machine. I knew nothing about motorbikes and couldn't have told a Kawasaki 500 from a Honda 50; all I knew was that they were invariably noisy, and that young men drove them too fast and got themselves killed. Not, to be fair, that this machine looked likely to be shattering anyone's peace, or risking anyone's neck, in its delivery condition. It was covered in grime and had the disused, rust-encrusted appearance of something that had been stored away and forgotten about in someone's barn for years (which in fact turned out to be almost exactly the case). It was padlocked to the bottom of the cast-iron fire escape that ran down the back of the flats from our kitchen doors (though why anyone should think such a relic of interest to thieves I couldn't imagine) and from then on Harry could be found during most of the daylight hours tinkering and clanking on the concrete under the steps, with bits of the motorbike scattered around him, the back door wide open, and music issuing at full blast. Ah well, I thought, men will be boys, and after one mortifying experience made a mental note not to wear a skirt when I took the rubbish down.

I saw little of them during the summer vacation, mostly because I wasn't around much. I went to Greece for the first month with my boyfriend Chris, which was hot and fun, and Chris was very relaxed and carefree, and hardly made any spiteful remarks about his ex-wife. Though he did take dozens of photographs, which I suspected would get shown to his daughters when we returned home, in the hope that they would be reported back to Alyssia. Evidence of the wonderful bachelor existence he was enjoying without her.

I should say something about Chris. He, of course, was Mrs Rosen's 'good-looking boy'. He was indeed good looking, tall and blond and willowy and even quite graceful when he wasn't trying to do anything practical, but he was not a boy. He was thirty-three, that summer. He taught English at my college and we'd been lovers since the previous September. (He was separated and divorced by then – I never knew him as a married man.) Chris wasn't perfect as a partner but what I liked about him was that, despite his anger with Alyssia, he seemed to sincerely like women. He'd first attracted my interest when I'd heard him tell a male student that his favourite authors were Mrs Gaskell, Barbara Pym, and Alison Lurie. Hey, I thought, impressed; that could be my list. And he was civilized without being pompous, or toeing any lines. I'd properly fallen for him when we'd toured the Tate Gallery together. After two hours cruising the halls he'd stopped me at a doorway and directed my gaze back into the near-empty room. At the far end a punkish boy and girl dressed entirely in black and silver were resting back-to-back on a bench, framed by a huge red canvas on the end wall. Chris smiled and murmured, 'Actually, I think that makes the most stunning picture here.' And after staring at the couple I'd just had to kiss him, because I thought he was thrillingly right, and shared moments like that jump you straight to intimacy.

So that summer Chris was, to me, a like-minded companion, close friend, and attractive lover. To him I was all these things (at least I hope I was) but in addition – and this could be a source of friction – I was also a potential wife, because a wife was what he really wanted, and because he liked to view all relationships as 'going somewhere'. Even, most regrettably, relationships that had got there once and were now bitterly limping back. Occasionally, when I was at his place, perhaps lying in bed while he wandered around with coffee mugs, I'd catch him looking at me with an expression that said as clearly as if it were written on his forehead, 'If only she could see me now, she'd be sorry.' It's unpleasant to be used as a weapon by anyone, and it was another friction between us, even if it was so patently a useless or imaginary weapon. Alyssia, I felt sure, would have been delighted and relieved to see evidence that he was rebuilding his life. She left him, after all. But I've heard it said that the happiest members of society are single childless women in their early thirties, and the unhappiest unmarried men of the same age, and I can well believe it. There was something almost desperate about Chris's yearning for domesticity. What he really needed was a nice younger woman who'd give him a whole new family, and to whom he could once again play husband and father. What he didn't need, given those requirements, was me; but on the other hand at the time he did need someone, and I was more than willing, in my own limited way, so he put his faith in the power of conversion, and dived straight in.

And for those four weeks in Greece our differences were forgotten anyway. There was only sun, sea, wine, sex and strangers; so he shrugged off past and future, and I rarely saw myself as weapon, or wife.

Then after Greece I went up to Norwich for three weeks, to stay with my sister Berry and her husband Brian, partly as a holiday and partly to babysit for the children while Berry and Brian were at work. I did it every summer, so they didn't have to use up all their holiday in child care and could get away for a week or two as a family. Brian thought this behaviour of mine suspect in its altruism, but I got stacks of holiday, I love Berry and the kids, and since she was providing the future generation that I felt I could have some sort of stake in, having left it a bit late to start one of my own, I saw nothing odd in repaying her with a little of my time. That Brian had difficulties seeing me in the benevolently self-sacrificing role traditional to maiden aunts was, in my view, entirely his problem.

In mid-September, less than a fortnight after I'd got back from Norwich, everyone in the flats received notices to quit. The letter – headed 'Dear Tenant', so I knew it wasn't just me – informed us that the block had been sold to a consortium, and awaited our response. I experienced a moment's heart-stopping jolt before commonsense prevailed and I tossed the letter to one side, knowing we had security of tenure, and that this was just a meaningless try-on. A mischievous try-on, however, and it occurred to me immediately that some of the other tenants might not be so sure of their rights. I had visions of mass panic setting in across the way. When the bell rang I knew before I opened the door that it would be Mrs Rosen – I'd never seen her so excited. I tried reassurances but she wasn't listening to a word I said; she absolutely refused to be done out of her outrage. I could only get rid of her in the end by agreeing to call round that evening for a tenants' meeting at her flat, although I can't say I relished the prospect one bit.

These tenants' meetings happened only very infrequently. We were not a particularly united bunch, and I tended to remain on the fringe of what little community action there was, because I was so out on a limb, geographically speaking. But when we did have them they were always held in the Rosens' flat, which had to be the least suitable of all venues, since there was scarcely space in their sitting room for all the furniture they possessed, never mind a dozen or so adults and one child.

In fact on this occasion we were slightly under strength, because the Williams' grown-up son cried off with a heavy cold – wise decision, I thought – and Mrs Gardiner left Louise in bed with the front door open in case she called, but even so it was like playing sardines. Smoked sardines at that, because Mr Rosen then insisted on lighting up his foul-smelling pipe, sickly-sweet traces of which lingered over him even when you met him in the street, as if he'd got a very dead animal in the process of cremation tucked under his jacket.

I was surprised to see both Ruth and Harry there. I had imagined that someone like Harry would consider a get-together like this way beneath him; but there he was, propped inconspicuously against the wall by the window, leaving the enormous and hideous three-piece suite (tasselled purple velour – you could see royalty enthroned on it) and assorted pouffes for the older generations. He gave me no acknowledgement, though Ruth, when I caught her eye, responded with a brief smile. I took a chair as near as possible to the open door, a position which had the added advantage of being within chatting distance of the aged Mrs Bundy, a splendid old lady whom I liked enormously and who despised Mrs Rosen even more than I did.

As it turned out, Harry and Ruth made the only sensible suggestions of the evening, which lasted much longer than it needed because Mrs Rosen felt impelled to repeat every comment anybody else made as if doing a simultaneous translation for some hidden and hard-of-hearing audience, imbuing each repetition with scorn or cordiality, depending on whether the utterer was in her good books or bad. I contributed nothing for once, except in mocking asides to Mrs Bundy. Somehow Ruth and Harry's presence inhibited me, perhaps because I didn't want to be associated with the ludicrous ramblings emanating from some of the other tenants. Normally they exasperated me so much that I was forced into speech, if only to counter the more ridiculous scare-mongering that got bandied about.

Harry's sensible suggestion was that we open the window. Indeed it wasn't really a suggestion at all, more a unilateral action. He simply muttered, 'I'll open the window, shall I?' and since he was standing right by it, did it, without waiting for a reply. Several of us turned to him through the fug with grateful smiles – no one had ever dared propose such a thing before. Mrs Rosen fixed him with an affronted glare, but it was done by then and she could hardly march up and close it, particularly since there was no way she could physically reach that part of the room without scrambling over a mountain of furniture and bodies.

And then Ruth, who had been sitting quietly till then, no doubt savouring her first taste of grass-roots dynamics, must have decided she'd had enough.

'Actually,' she said, cutting through an argument about council house queue-jumping by blacks, which had somehow become embroiled in the issue, 'I don't think we need to do anything at all. If you like I'll type out a standard letter saying we all want to take advantage of the Rent Act, and . . .

well . . .' she smiled around the room almost apologetically '. . . that should be that.'

I guessed Mrs Rosen regarded this impertinence as even more offensive than Harry's. However, it was immediately greeted with cries of 'What d'you mean?' and 'How d'you know, dear?' and followed, after Ruth had explained, by a chorus of 'Oh, how wonderful!' and 'Isn't she clever!' and 'Would you really, dear?' Then everybody started talking at once, a sure sign the meeting was over, and before Mrs Rosen could restore order to voice any objection we were all getting up to go.

I walked back across the grass with Harry and Ruth. Ruth said something like, 'My God, are they always like that?' and I replied drily, 'Worse, usually,' and she laughed and invited me in for coffee. And that was the first time I had been in their flat in the four months they had been there.

It's odd, going into a flat that is identical to your own except for the furnishings. A disorienting mixture of familiar and alien, all the more alien somehow because of the underlying familiarity. I decided, looking round their sitting room, that neither of them could be very interested in the aesthetics of a home. The furniture – though mercifully sparse, a positive relief after what we'd just left – was a hotch-potch of styles, leaving the impression that either they weren't very sure of their tastes, or that they were, but those tastes were very different and they hadn't discovered compromise. A brown twill sofa, for instance, though pleasant enough in itself, looked quite out of place on the faded reds and blues of a rather beautiful Indian carpet. And the issue had been avoided altogether on the walls, which were completely bare except for bookshelves and a long mirror I passed in the hall; not a picture, print, poster or plate to be seen.

Harry made the coffee and I stayed with them for the rest of the evening, catching up on news we should have exchanged months before. I liked Ruth immediately. It's difficult to describe someone you wholeheartedly like and admire without gushing; I'll say only that from the start I sensed she was a better person than I am. More intelligent, less selfish, and much less cynical. But she has the knack of making people around her feel good too, so I've never resented her for it, and a flip sense of humour that keeps her reassuringly this side of perfect. I used to wonder how her nature survived her job, until I swapped the words around and grasped that that was why she did the job at all.

Of course we didn't get to any great intimacy that first evening. The questions I really wanted answers to, like 'How on earth did you two meet?' and 'Why doesn't he work?' were quite unaskable at this early stage. We didn't get much further than her job and mine, where they'd lived before (Kemp Town, Brighton) and what they'd discovered about the local area. It turned out that they both knew London pretty well; better than me, probably. I didn't move here till university and I didn't have a car, so London to me was a collection of urban villages linked by underground tunnels, except for those strips I was familiar with from the local buses. They didn't have a car either, but Harry had apparently spent a year in London despatch riding when he was nineteen (a quick calculation put him now at twenty-seven) and Ruth said she was born in Finchley and lived there until her parents moved to Chichester, when she was fourteen, so North London at least must have been old territory to her.

At one point she left the room to make more coffee and go to the bathroom, and Harry and I were left alone. He had distributed cups early on – rather formally, I thought, as if obeying strict orders – but to the conversation following had contributed nothing. I couldn't think of anything to say to him; jobs are so useful as talking points – any question I thought of seemed to connect itself to the fact that he didn't have one, and since I didn't know whether his unemployment was a matter of choice or fate I preferred not to raise the subject myself. And it didn't look as if any initiative was going to come from him. After a brainracking silence I suddenly remembered the bike, and just as Ruth re-entered the room asked how it was coming along.

He stared at me a moment, as if debating whether I was genuinely interested, or might have an ulterior motive for asking. I felt rather as I did addressing my more truculent male students: about ninety, and beyond hope. Finally he said, 'Slowly.'

Ruth sat down. She was wearing jeans, but still twisted her legs sideways, knees close together, in the way women do when they are accustomed to wearing skirts.

'It'd come on a lot faster,' she said, smiling, 'if he wasn't such a perfectionist.'

'Or if I had a place to work on it,' he said, in a tone suggesting that lack of space for mechanical operations was a minor bone of contention.

'What is it anyway?' I asked politely. Having raised the topic it seemed tactless to jettison it the moment Ruth reappeared. 'It looks pretty old.'

He said it was an AJS 500 circa 1956 and had belonged to his father. The make meant nothing to me but I knew the British motorcycle industry was at best moribund if not extinct, and enquired how he managed for spares. He shrugged and replied, 'With difficulty,' after which I decided I'd persevered long enough.

Ruth commented that I hadn't been around much in the summer, and I explained where I had been, and then somehow the conversation drifted round to, or rather hovered over, the fact that I lived alone. I was a little sensitive about this, even though I knew I had no reason to be. But it was surprising how many people unthinkingly made remarks that implied my situation was an inherently regrettable one, and therefore one I must have been reduced to, or forced into, and not an option I might conceivably have chosen of my own free will. Several of my friends, on seeing the size of my flat (the flats did seem impressively spacious on entering, seven doors off the hall, even if one was only the airing cupboard) had asked why I didn't get a flatmate, either with a note of disapproval, as if there was something vaguely reprehensible about a woman occupying quite so much space on her own, or helpfully, as if women were creatures who could only thrive in close proximity to others, with whom they could share the intimate minutiae of their lives. In both cases there was an undertone of pity, an unspoken assumption that whatever arrangement I came to it was anyway only second best; first best being naturally the ideal state of living with a man.

And yet I saw the choice I'd made as not only sensible, but actually essential. (And as far as flatmates were concerned, if I didn't want the bother of considering other people's needs in the privacy of my home, and could afford to do without them, then that was my business.) I had lived with men in the past, my judgement clouded by the optimism of romantic love, but I had never felt the desire to marry, or bear the children of my lovers. (I'd only have married for children and early on decided to have them only if I experienced definite longings, which never came.) So when the relationships ended, as perhaps they were more likely to given those constraints, the conflict was immeasurably intensified and protracted by the complication of achieving physical separation; indeed on the last occasion I'd ended up losing not only my lover and my home but also, because of my reluctance to engage in out-and-out warfare, most of my possessions. After that experience I made up my mind that whatever else I did in life I would never again be tempted to give up the security and continuity of my own home. This decision seemed to me both reasonable and practical; I found it astonishing how difficult it appeared to be for some people to comprehend. I even argued about it occasionally with Chris, who should have known better than most about the risks of impermanence in relationships. It was, naturally, my flat he wanted us to dispose of, and not his house; easy for him to suggest, and even easier for me to reject.

Of course I didn't say all this to Ruth and Harry. I merely said that I enjoyed living alone, that I'd tried flatshares (true: in the distant past and even briefly the previous year, when I'd provided a two-month bolt hole for Joanna, one of Berry's friends) and that although the experiences had been tolerable they'd nevertheless confirmed my conviction that I wasn't cut out for communal living. I didn't say much more, because at that point I realized I needn't have said anything at all; though the conversation had veered towards it, the questions had never actually been asked.

To shift the subject – and mentally kicking myself for exposing chips – I told Ruth I had a boyfriend who stayed occasionally. 'Oh the fair man; I've seen him,' she nodded, and a few minutes later casually suggested going out as a foursome some time he was over. I agreed just as vaguely, so neither of us would feel committed to anything. I could see that Chris would like Ruth, but Harry? Or perhaps (such are our foolish thoughts) Harry was more relaxed with men, as some men are.

It transpired that 'relaxed' was not the word I meant, because soon afterwards it became apparent that Harry was having no difficulty relaxing with me. His chair was turned away from us so he could rest his feet on an alcove stereo table, but I could see enough of his face in profile – the upper half, crucially – to ascertain that he had fallen asleep. I couldn't think why he should be so tired, considering the absolute nothing he did all day, and was mildly offended that I could be so ignorable.

Ruth noticed his unconsciousness a moment later and waved a hand dismissively in his direction, as if this was a normal occurrence when she was entertaining friends (as it may well have been – words weren't action in Harry's view, and nothing less could keep him awake for long).

But I had already glanced at my watch and realized the evening was over.

## Chapter 2

A fortnight later my flat was burgled.

I came home from work about five, passed the sounds of rock music in the lobby and arrived at my own front door to find it ajar and the reinforced glass smashed and scattered all over the floor. Through the half-open door I could see things – my things, though unrecognizable as such – strewn across the rucked and glinting carpet. For a moment I was completely disoriented. It even entered my mind that I was at the wrong door, and I actually checked the number below the smashed glass with a lunatic hope that I had been mistaken. I didn't go in; I couldn't. I turned on the spot and walked, and then ran, down the stairs, and hammered on Ruth and Harry's door.

I must have looked as shocked as I felt; the moment Harry opened up he said, 'What's wrong?' and glanced up and down the lobby sharply, as if hopeful that whatever was wrong was still lurking nearby.

I said, 'My front door's smashed in,' and suddenly had to put down the shopping bags I was still idiotically clutching.

'Shit,' he muttered, and without waiting to arm himself – I realized my retreat from the flat had been hastened by the horrible thought that although I had heard nothing there might just have been someone there – he bounded up the stairs.

I left the shopping bags outside their door and walked slowly up behind him. My brain was still misfiring and at first-floor level a wild notion flicked through it: that I'd been broken into not by burglars but by Joanna's ex-husband. My temporary flatmate of the previous winter had been bolting primarily – and with very good reason – from him. Then just as quickly the notion crumbled; because he was, I knew, safely in prison.

At the doorway of the flat I caught Harry emerging from my bedroom into the hall, looking almost disappointed.

'Jesus, what a mess,' he said, and then, glancing at me, 'It's OK. Nobody around.'

I walked into the hall and froze. I'd heard friends who'd been burgled say they felt violated, but I didn't feel that. Not then, anyway. I simply felt numb. I couldn't think what to do, or where to start. It looked like a pack effort. They'd even been through the kitchen cupboards, ferociously, and half the unit doors hung out into the room at crazy angles. I didn't want to look anywhere else, and especially not in my bedroom. Somehow it didn't occur to me to worry about what had been stolen; it was the mess I couldn't cope with.

'Bloody kids,' Harry murmured, and with a shake of his head stopped me picking up a table lamp by my feet.

I looked around in despair, knowing that even if I shouldn't be doing that, I should be doing something.

He gave me ten seconds to grapple with this insoluble dilemma, and then said, 'There's nothing you can do here. We'll ring the police from downstairs.'

I nodded blindly and turned for the door.

Downstairs Harry dealt with the action side of things. I didn't ask him to but he did anyway, and that was fine by me. He rang the police, made me a cup of tea, hung around the lobby waiting for police cars, and went up with the officers when they arrived. From the sitting room window I counted four, three in plain clothes, one in uniform. Harry had sounded pessimistic about getting one.

When I felt a little stronger I went up as well and started trying to work out what exactly had been taken, although it's extremely hard to remember what you do own, never mind what you don't any longer, and almost impossible when most of it has been tossed about the place like confetti.

There were some breakages – a lamp, a mirror and several plates – but fewer than I had feared, and none of possessions I particularly treasured; in the end all I could list as definitely missing was my portable cassette player and some costume jewellery, none of it valuable. I was wearing my only irreplaceable possession, my mother's amethyst ring, as I always did, against precisely such invasion.

A man who said he was a forensic officer took my finger-prints; to eliminate them, he said, from any others he came up with. While he was doing it, feeling slightly oppressed by the presence of so many large male strangers, I expressed my surprise that I merited so much attention.

'Regular crime wave round here,' one of the other plain clothes officers said over his shoulder. 'Twelfth break-in this week. You're a lucky one.'

'Ah,' I said. Lucky because I'd got them, I supposed.

When they'd done my fingerprints they said they wanted Harry's, but he swore he hadn't touched anything and had never been in the flat before, and eventually they gave up with him.

I received the strong impression, reinforced by this exchange, that Harry didn't like the police. He stayed in the flat but posted himself as close to the open front door as possible and volunteered nothing but watchful silence to the proceedings. When the policemen spoke to him he replied, but with extreme brevity, and with a kind of repressed stillness that created immediate tension in the air.

I thought his attitude unhelpful, though with these particular policemen, understandable. The uniformed bobby and the forensic officer were civil enough (in fact the latter reminded me endearingly of an old boyfriend, all heart under the tactless bonhomie and crass clichés) but the two CID men had downright unpleasant manners. They tramped around the flat as if they owned it, looking disconcertingly more like hard-nosed criminals than upholders of the law, addressed Harry patronizingly as 'my son', despite being themselves young men – certainly younger than I – and were positively offensive to him over the fingerprint issue. His explanation that he must have been asleep or listening to loud music while the crime was committed above him was greeted with frank contempt. During my own interview with them they didn't smile once, they were impatient and exasperated with my hesitancy over what had been stolen, and ended up reprimanding me because I hadn't got a deadlock, so that the thieves had only to smash the glass and reach in to turn the Yale.

I did appreciate that to them the whole exercise must have seemed a complete waste of time, and that they saw hundreds of similar scenes every year, but I didn't and it was my flat, and I felt they should have shown more consideration. I rarely cry, and certainly not in front of strange men, but I was close to it by the end of their lecture. Not that they appeared to notice, being at the time more interested in outglaring Harry, whom they would have clearly loved to arrest, if only for persistent obstinacy.

Harry, however, I think did; I was aware of his approach, and then a restlessness beside me, until finally he cut in to ask if they'd got all they needed.

Grudgingly, they admitted they had.

'Right,' he said shortly, 'we'll go back downstairs.'

It surprised me that no one objected; the place had been taken over so effectively it was hard to believe we were free to go. But no one said anything, and when Harry asked the forensic officer to bang on the front door downstairs when they'd finished he agreed without any hint in his voice that the request was out of order. So we left.

Downstairs in the lobby we met Ruth. She was walking backwards through the double doors, staring at the police cars parked on the pavement outside.

We gave her the news.

'Oh, Jane,' she said, with such distress that it choked me up again. All I could do was nod.

'What you need,' she said, guiding me firmly into the flat, 'is a good strong drink.'

This turned out to be whisky, which I didn't normally drink, but was only too happy to on this occasion. Then after a couple of stiff ones Ruth said we might as well eat, as the police cars were still outside, so we spun two gammon rashers out between three, and filled the gaps with Brie and Boursin from the shopping I'd left in their hall.

As we were finishing, the police knocked to say they were leaving. The whisky and food had restored my spirits considerably. I'd even begun to feel relieved that the burglary hadn't been worse. Not much had been broken or stolen, and they hadn't slashed the curtains, or defecated on the carpets. A few hours tidying up and things wouldn't seem so bad. As soon as I heard the lobby doors slam I stood up.

'I've got to make a start on it,' I said. 'I can't leave it like that.'

'We'll give you a hand,' Ruth said matter of factly. She looked across at Harry.

'Sure,' he said, with no discernible lack of enthusiasm.

I protested – they'd done enough already, it seemed to me – but Ruth was adamant. Harry didn't back her up, but seemed willing to do whatever she decided. So we refilled our glasses, loaded up with my shopping bags, and trooped upstairs.

The police presence had not improved the mess. However, viewed through several whiskies and alongside two other people it seemed less depressing.

By tacit agreement I took the bedroom, leaving Ruth the sitting room, and Harry the kitchen and hall. (I was searching for rarely used implements for months afterwards, but he achieved a quite unaccustomary neatness and managed to get the unit doors back on, plus he didn't keep asking where everything went, which is so wearing.)

We closed the door on the third room, which I used as a study, to be dealt with later. The thieves hadn't shown much interest in paperwork, and since there wasn't much else to attract them the mess there was relatively undaunting. The bathroom and lavatory were thankfully untouched, though, inexplicably, clothes had been tossed around in the airing cupboard.

While on my hands and knees in the bedroom, scraping together a spilt jarful of ornamental pebbles, I spotted my old silver trinket box under the bed and was relieved I hadn't reported it missing earlier. I imagined the thieves hurling it there in disgust after discovering that all it contained was a diaphragm cap and spermicidal jelly. It was empty, but groping further under the bed I found the tube of jelly, and then the cap itself, nestling in a clump of underbed fluff. I held it up to the light for evidence of handling and saw none, but decided to replace it anyway. (I always used the cap; Chris used to complain that it was messy, and certainly it must be the noisiest form of contraception around, but I always thought that made sex rather more fun. If he was prepared to use a

condom I did without, but he always chose the first packet
that came to hand because his vocal cords became paralysed
in chemist shops, and multi-coloured condoms with knobs
on caused a lot more hysteria than the odd swamp-like
squelch ever did.)

When the flat was more or less back to normal Ruth
approached me and asked if I would like to spend the night
with her downstairs. I'd heard her a minute ago, exchanging
quiet words with Harry in the kitchen. She glanced at him,
now propped against the door jamb, and added, 'Harry will
stay up here if you like, while the place is insecure.'

I shook my head. It had already briefly occurred to me to
go over to Chris's, but now the flat was habitable again I
positively wanted to stay. To re-assert my ownership, make
it mine again.

'Thanks,' I said, 'but I want to stay. It would only be
putting it off. I'll nail something over the front door.'

In fact the smashed glass had slipped my mind till then. I
wasn't even sure I possessed a nail, never mind something to
cover the hole. But I knew I wanted to stay and wasn't going
to let the problem of the door stand in my way.

Harry flicked his eyes at Ruth, who was looking dubious,
shrugged, and said, 'It's OK. I'll do it. Won't take long.'

He disappeared downstairs and returned a minute later
with two short planks, a cardboard box, and several stout
nails. With the planks and cardboard in place the front door
looked as if I was preparing for a major siege, but at least no
one could see in any more, and it was probably as robust as
the glass had been, even if that had given a greater illusion of
security. While he was finishing it off he reminded me about
the deadlock.

'Yes,' I said vaguely, not quite sure what such an instal-
lation would involve.

'The ironmongers on the High Road,' he insisted. 'They do them. And glass.'

I frowned. 'Isn't the front door the landlord's responsibility?'

He banged in the last nail. 'Christ,' he sighed. 'If you want to wait till they get round to it you'll still have this at Christmas. And they won't fit a mortise for you. Just get it done and bill them. They might cough up.'

He turned to look at me. I detested having to organize jobs like this and it must have shown. He smiled, somewhat patronizingly. 'Look,' he said, 'leave me the keys and some cash and I'll do it tomorrow morning. It's not difficult.' He thought. 'Say twenty. Glass is bloody expensive.'

Why not, I thought tiredly, if he was offering, and it was apparently so incredibly easy? I couldn't face the alternative: going through the yellow pages and then making elaborate arrangements to be in when the workmen arrived, which of course they wouldn't until I'd given up and gone out somewhere. I'd been through it before with television repair men and the like, and the rage it induced was insupportable.

'Well, if you're sure . . .' I said, though I knew I wasn't giving him a chance not to be. I didn't care. But I told him I'd take the morning off anyway, to simplify matters. Burglary was quite enough excuse.

So it was settled, and Harry said he'd be round first thing in the morning with a tape to measure up. I thanked them both sincerely for their help and when they had gone picked up the phone to ring Chris. It was almost midnight but I wanted to talk to him.

After only one ring his voice said, 'Yes?', sounding abrupt rather than sleepy. I guessed he was already in bed – he had a bedside extension – but that I hadn't woken him.

'It's me,' I said. 'I've been burgled.'

'Christ!' I could hear him shifting position – swinging his legs out of bed, maybe. 'Burgled? Are you all right?'

'Yes. Well, as all right as you can be after being trampled over by a squad of policemen. I got home to find the place turned over. Awful mess. But the couple downstairs have helped clear up. Nothing much was stolen . . .'

'How did they get in?'

'Smashed the front door glass. I've had to have it boarded over.'

'Jesus, Jane. You should have rung me . . .'

He sounded so appalled I had to suppress an impulse to laugh. 'I am ringing you,' I said, smiling.

'Earlier,' he said reprovingly. There was a moment's silence. Then in a deeply protective tone he said, 'You must be very shaken up. Would you like me to come over?'

'Oh, no,' I said. I was touched, though – it was a fair drive from his place. 'It's much too late. You're in bed. I just wanted to tell you I won't be in college till the afternoon.'

'No, right. But it'd be no trouble. Really. I could be with you before one.'

'No, honestly, I'm fine.' I was suddenly entertained by a vision of Chris wrestling with the lobby doors at one in the morning – they always pretended they were locked although they weren't – and then being confronted by a vigilant and menacing Harry, who would knock him senseless before he had a chance to explain himself. Heartened by this evidence of mental recovery I repeated, 'I'm fine. I'll see you after lunch.'

'Sure?' he said.

'Quite sure. I'll tell you about it then. And come back for dinner afterwards,' I added. 'If you can, that is.'

Dinner invitations always included breakfast too. Chris said quietly, 'Of course I can.'

We spoke for a couple more minutes and rang off the best of friends.

At nine o'clock the next morning Harry turned up at my front door bearing tool box and tape, looking frightfully masculine and efficient. He measured up the door and then disappeared with one of my cheques, because I hadn't got enough cash. Personally I didn't think the shop would accept it, not without me and my banker's card, but he was airily optimistic; evidently he'd used the place a lot and was a recognizable face there to whom they would refuse nothing.

I was feeling much better after a night's sleep. Indeed at moments – perhaps it's a natural stage of the recovery process – quite aggressively positive. While I waited for Harry to return I made a start on the study, and at one point found myself actually humming aloud, as I recollected that my insurance policy was New-for-Old, meaning I might even profit from the affair. And a little later, just after spotting Harry on the pavement below, triumphantly bearing an awkwardly large and heavy sheet of glass, I recalled the annoying tendency of the cassette player to chew up my tapes. I hoped it chewed up a lot of the burglars'. Serve them right.

We did the glass first; a fiddly business, because of having to remove the old jagged pieces safely. We bundled them up in sheaves of old newspaper and stuffed them into a black plastic rubbish sack. As I taped a large Broken Glass label on to it for the dustmen, I remembered the last occasion I'd issued such a public-spirited warning (not glass that time but the razor-sharp guts of a collapsed armchair) and grinned to myself. I'd given the warning verbally and as reward received a five-minute eulogy from the extremely handsome and friendly West Indian foreman, plus an unsolicited glimpse of his rubbish-scarred legs.

Fitting the new glass didn't require my assistance, apparently, so I fetched a chair from the kitchen and sat on it at the back of the hall to watch. I asked if Harry minded an audience, although I'm not sure why; it would have been even ruder to have shut myself in another room, as if he were a paid workman.

'Your flat, be my guest,' he murmured, and gave a snort of amusement as the contradiction registered.

I sat there, studying the process closely – it could happen again, after all, and I might not always have such helpful neighbours – and soon realized I was enjoying myself. It's a pleasure to watch anyone doing a job well, making it look so easy. I tried to imagine Chris doing this – I couldn't bear to see him even re-wiring a plug, he was so hamfisted – and smiled to myself envisaging the carnage. And he would have ended up in a vile temper, because he hated inanimate objects getting the better of him, which they always did. It would save a lot of frayed nerves, I thought, if that young wife he was going to get one day turned out to be a skilled handy-woman; and car mechanic too, while she was at it. Chris had never got to practical grips with the simplest workings of the internal combustion engine – to his own exorbitant cost – even if he could bluff his way through the rudiments at the college bar.

I complimented Harry on his workmanship, and he replied, 'Yeah, well,' absently, as if his standards were far removed from those of a mere female dilettante. There were long periods of silence, but not an uncomfortable silence, because he was busy and absorbed, and I was interested and impressed.

While he was tapping in the last of the wooden beading strips round the glass I skimmed through the instructions for the mortise lock. It seemed to entail a fair bit of digging out of wood, but otherwise seemed surprisingly straight-forward. Because I didn't want Harry to think I was completely incompetent – I had been known to put up shelves in the past, though admittedly the distant past, and with a borrowed drill – I felt compelled to comment on the apparent simplicity of the operation. And even to hazard the opinion that given the tools I could probably do it myself.

Harry shot me a hard look over his shoulder, reached down to pick out the wood chisel and hammer from the tool box and silently held them out to me.

I laughed, knowing it wasn't a serious challenge, and genuinely entertained.

He smiled back, enjoying the joke, a completely unguarded, natural smile, and it felt like a breakthrough: our first spontaneously friendly exchange. Of course he'd been kind the night before, and I'd been grateful, but this mild teasing struck an entirely new, familiar note. As I trotted into the kitchen to prepare for the more female chores of a job like this, such as making the tea and fetching the dustpan and brush, I thought triumphantly: we've cracked it, we're actually getting somewhere, he doesn't dislike me after all; and was astounded at how readily, in the glow of this, I was prepared to forgive him the discourtesies of the past.

When I returned to the hall I asked him, in keeping with the new spirit of friendship, how the bike was coming along.

'Fair bit to do yet.' He stopped what he was doing and turned to look at me. 'You don't know anyone with garage space or a workshop round here, do you? I'm going to need somewhere soon.' He picked up the socket section of the mortise and started marking the door jamb where it had to be sunk in. 'I tried to persuade Ruth to hand over the dining room for the winter but she's not having it. There must be somewhere round here.'

Good heavens, I thought, in automatic sympathy with Ruth over such an outrageous request. Not that I could think of anywhere else, except the back yard boiler house. It was fairly big – big enough to store coal, in pre-oilfired days – and I knew the part-time caretaker kept tools there. Convenient, too, jutting out between their flat and the Rosens'. But he'd already considered and rejected it.

'Too dark, and not secure. I need somewhere I can lay things out and leave them. Kids are in and out of there all the time.'

I laughed and said jokingly, 'Shame you can't get it up the fire escape into the empty flat. Bags of space there. I've been tempted to store junk there myself.'

He looked up sharply. 'Why? You got a key?'

I hesitated. I did, as it happened, but I wasn't at all sure I wanted the fact known. The couple who'd lived there last had given me a spare when they left so I could forward on their post. Although I hadn't been down for months; nothing but circulars in the last few batches. Still, I didn't seriously believe Harry could get several hundredweight of bike up there.

Reluctantly I said, 'Well, yes, but . . .'

He tapped the door jamb in front of him thoughtfully.

'But you couldn't get the bike up there,' I objected.

'Wouldn't need to,' he said, still thinking. 'It's space to strip the engine down I want. I could get the engine up.'

'But well . . . suppose the agents found out . . ? Wouldn't it be illegal?' I wondered what Ruth would think of the idea: she, at least, I presumed, had to be careful.

'Doubt it,' he said. 'Not if I got in with a key and didn't nick any electricity.' He shrugged. 'Who's to know, anyway? No one's been near the place since we've been here.'

This, I thought, was probably true. I suspected he might be right about the legality too, but it still felt wrong.

He said, 'Can we take a look when I've finished this?' and turned away from me to resume work.

I stared at his back, feeling trapped. He glanced round,

looking for my answer, and since I didn't see how I could say no, I said yes. I went into the kitchen to dig out the key from a drawer, and after he had raced through the final stages and demonstrated how perfectly the deadlock worked (which I never doubted, but it seemed to give him some pleasure – and leverage, too, as he was no doubt aware) I led the way downstairs.

The front door of the flat swept a small mountain of post across the boards as it swung open, but all circulars or brown buff, nothing personal. I bent down to stash it into a pile, briefly debating whether to dispose of it in the bin upstairs or post it back through the door after we left, to look convincing. Although I doubted a casual inspection would notice the absence of something.

'I could work in here,' Harry's voice called, from the back bedroom.

I sighed and joined him. Bare painted boards, hessian wallpaper: without furniture the room looked half the size of my bedroom upstairs.

'No risk of being overlooked,' Harry said. We both peered out through the window. Nothing to be seen except the dustbin strip of the scruffy back yard, and, beyond, the lush gardens of the big houses in The Avenue. He slid the lower sash up a fraction. 'I could run an extension up from downstairs. Hey, great.' He gazed around the room with satisfaction.

I felt deeply uncomfortable. I wanted him to use the place, but not through me.

Harry was always good at reading minds. Compensation, perhaps, for his shortcomings in the more conventional modes of communication.

'I won't involve you,' he said. I hadn't said a word, but he made it sound as if I had. 'And I'll be careful. If I need lighting I'll black the windows out. It'd only be for a couple of months.'

He'd have got it anyway, I think, but the assurances made it easier. As I handed the key over I said sternly, 'Get your own cut from that, and give me mine back. If it comes to it I shall deny all knowledge of yours. You can say you found it in your flat. OK?'

'Right.' He nodded down at it obediently, trying to look serious and responsible, but missing both by a mile. He stopped trying, and released a jubilant grin.

Looking at him I thought: what a Jekyll and Hyde you are, Harry, and wondered if he knew how off-putting he appeared when he was a stranger and unknown, and, if so, what drove him to project such an image when he was clearly not an unpleasant person underneath. In fact at that precise moment I felt almost tender towards him, the tenderness one feels handing a child the present he has been yearning for passionately, and witnessing his undisguisable delight.

I grinned back at him, and, in case he could read those thoughts too, turned away.

# Chapter 3

The next day I went to see Joanna. This had nothing to do with the burglary; except, perhaps, that two reminders are more effective than one. The first reminder, of course, had been those fleeting thoughts on discovering the break-in; the second was the arrival that morning of two letters: one a fairly bulky object for Joanna, the other wafer thin but otherwise identical, for me.

My letter – posted first class, unlike Joanna's – was from Aitken and Drew, Joanna's Norwich-based solicitors, and was nothing more than a one-page apology for my receipt of her letter. An inexperienced member of staff, it said, had failed to notice Joanna's change of address and the error had not been spotted until the enclosures were already posted. I knew what they meant by 'enclosures'; they acted as Joanna's accommodation address, and they meant letters to her from anyone who hadn't been told where she'd escaped to when she'd left Norwich; i.e. practically everyone. She hadn't even – at least at the time she'd been staying with me – told her own mother.

I could, of course, have simply forwarded the bulky letter on, as I'd done with all her post the previous winter, before Joanna had got round to giving the solicitors her new address. I'd even, I'm ashamed to say, have preferred to do this. (It's hard admitting, even to yourself, that someone you have profound sympathy for, and know to be deeply deserving of support, is nevertheless someone whose company you would not freely choose.) But guilt is a powerful force, as is the articulation of intent; the moment I saw the letters I groaned, 'God, I must go and see her,' and Chris heard me from the kitchen (we'd kept our dinner/breakfast date) and 'Who?'

'Joanna,' I said, and with a determination definitely strengthened by his presence checked my diary and decided to do it that very evening, before the impulse faded.

Joanna lived in a bedsit out at Archway. An impossible journey by public transport from Kilburn, but straightforward from work. She wasn't on the phone, so I couldn't forewarn her, but I thought that if I timed my arrival for 6.30ish I'd maximize my chances of finding her in. (And if I didn't, a weasly voice whispered, I'd have nothing to reproach myself for.) My afternoon sessions finished at four that day, but I spent an hour helping two of my more Neanderthal male students fill in Securicor job applications – please take them, I wrote invisibly on the forms, these boys are natural deterrents – and spent half an hour recovering with a woman friend in the canteen before setting off just before six.

I was almost too early; I actually met Joanna as we both emerged from Archway tube station. I was following a small, neat figure in an unfashionable salmon-pink coat and as she turned right out on to the pavement I saw her face, doll-like under the faded blond hair, and realized who it was.

'Joanna!' I said, hurrying to catch up with her.

She turned, blank-faced, and then as recognition dawned gave me a polite smile.

'Hello,' she said, though without turning fully towards me. She looked for a disconcerting moment as if she was about to walk on.

'I've come to see you,' I said quickly. Had she really been going to hurry away from me; someone she'd lived with for two months? The expression on her heavily made-up face was, as so often, impenetrable. 'Your solicitor sent me some post. By mistake. I thought I'd deliver it in person.' I smiled at her; I'd jumped at the chance, I hoped it said.

'Oh.' Joanna glanced down at my hands as if expecting me to be holding the letters, then looked up again. 'How nice,' she said, reassuming the polite smile. 'You must come back. We'll have some tea.'

We walked, swapping pleasantries, the half-mile to her bedsit. Joanna and I were the same age, give or take a year, yet beside her I felt – as I always did – that we belonged to different generations. Joanna, I always felt, belonged to a generation – or maybe a subset within one – whose life was built around manners and appearances; who shrank from intimacy, because it counted as 'troubling' people, and whose conventional shell had existed so long, and been clung to so fiercely, that it had ended up imprisoning more than protecting. I felt towards her as I might have towards a timid, unassuming, but ultimately iron-willed elderly relative – exasperated, despairing, but also, knowing what had caused her precariousness of self, compassionate. Joanna was the product of fifteen years of tyrannical and violent marriage, and whatever she could hold together now, I felt, she was entitled to.

Her bedsit was on the first floor of a gloomy smog-blackened house in a four-storey Victorian terrace. The original rooms must have been huge but were now partitioned into functional cubes. I'd been to the bedsit only once before, the day Joanna moved in. I remembered, vaguely, a darkish austere room with fine ceiling mouldings (though off-centre, because of the partitioning) and a kitchenette considerably taller, floor to ceiling, than its length or breadth. And I remembered too, fairly clearly, the battleship landlady who lived in the ground floor flat, whose nose I'd nearly rapped with my knuckles when she'd whipped the door open, anticipating my knock.

I saw the landlady again, very briefly, on this visit. 'Just a friend, Mrs E,' Joanna called down the stair well, to a massive aproned figure staring up from the shadowy hall at us. I heard a humphing grunt as the figure withdrew.

Joanna had – to my profound relief – taken the bedsit in hand. I could say, 'Hey, you've done wonders here,' with complete honesty. I shouldn't have been surprised: Joanna had always been a homemaker – obsessively so, reputedly, in the old days. Perhaps, with no children, her quest for self had manifested itself that way. But the room was now autumnally pastel, rather than dark – at least three vases of dried flowers underlined this – and fussily soft rather than austere, with scatter cushions and frills – all unquestionably feminine. It wasn't my taste, but it was someone's taste, and that was what I found so relieving.

Joanna took my jacket and waved me into one of two tweedy armchairs backing rather oddly, I thought, on to the glass of the room's huge sash window. She pulled up a small fabric-draped coffee table, carefully realigning the glossy women's magazines piled on it. Then took off her pink coat and hung it behind the door.

'How's work going?' I asked. She'd been temp-typing when she'd been with me.

'Oh . . .' She frowned at herself in a wall mirror to one side of the front door, patting at her blond bob. She shrugged. 'So so. You know . . .' She smiled back at me vaguely. 'Do you want tea or coffee?'

'Whatever you're having.' I tried again. 'Are you still with the same agency?'

'Um . . .' She was moving towards the kitchenette, pushing up the sleeves of her cream botany wool jersey. 'Sort of,'
she said over her shoulder, and disappeared.

While she was making whatever she'd decided on I dug out
her letter, and then occupied myself flicking through the top
pages of one of the women's magazines. I was very aware that
if Joanna had been a true woman friend I wouldn't be doing
this; I'd have been propped in the doorway to the kitchen,
probably with a snaffled biscuit in my hand, determined not to
waste a second of talking time.

After a minute or two I let fall the pages of the magazine and
listened. I could hear nothing. What was she doing in there?
Hiding? I felt suddenly irritable. Were either of us enjoying
this? I should have posted the letter.

I was about to rise – offer to help, anything, dammit – when
she reappeared at the doorway. She was bearing a wicker tray
on which was a floral teapot, matching crockery, and a plate of
biscuits.

I resettled myself in the chair and heard myself say, just as if
one of us was indeed a polite aged relative, 'Oh, you shouldn't
have gone to so much trouble.'

There's no answer to such a stupid remark and Joanna
sensibly didn't make one. She concentrated on lowering the
tray on to the table. Against the formality of the proceedings,
in this well-ordered, feminine room, it was impossible to
imagine her as a desperate victim of marital violence. Yet I
knew she had been. Her jaw and cheekbone had been broken
once, from a kick to the face. Maybe it wasn't actually
impossible to imagine; simply too painful to try.

After she had poured the tea and offered biscuits I complimented her again on the bedsit. How much lighter and cosier it
looked, very restful.

She nodded, looking around slowly. Then frowned and in a

slight rush said, 'I've been thinking of moving, actually.' She lowered her eyes, looking embarrassed. 'A little more space . . . um . . . you know.'

'Oh yes?' I was surprised. The room looked very settled. I wondered how much bigger a place she could possibly afford.

'Well.' Under her thick foundation I thought I detected a flush. 'Only thinking . . . Just . . . I don't expect I'll always be here.'

I'd said, 'Well no, obviously . . .' slightly baffled, before a mortifying thought struck me. Was I being paranoid, or was she in fact saying; don't assume I'll always be here, for you to drop in on? Good grief. I was momentarily hurt, and then – instantly forgiving her – appalled. It explained her vagueness about work, too. She was still frightened. Still running; even from me.

It made me remember the letter, which was sitting on the arm of my chair. I held it out to her. 'Don't forget this.'

She said, 'Oh yes,' in a faint voice and took it. She hesitated – I thought she was going to put it to one side to open later – but then she slipped a thumb nail under the seal and tore it open.

There were three letters inside, plus an Aitken and Drew compliment slip. The letters looked identical, cheap grey envelopes with hand-written addresses. Joanna stared at them, making no attempt to open them. I'd already recognized them – she'd had half a dozen or so during her stay with me – and knew exactly what was coming next.

She gave me a fixed half-smile and then tore each into halves, then quarters, then eighths. Her hands were trembling. How sacrosanct letters are; nobody, not her friends, not even her solicitors, would destroy her husband's letters to her.

I said, more as a statement than a question, 'He's still in prison then . . .'

'Oh yes.' She nodded abruptly. 'For a while yet. And I got my decree nisi months ago. He shouldn't be doing this.'

Her hands fluttered helplessly over the torn scraps littering her end of the coffee table. They were an invasion: even as unread scraps of paper, I could see that. And they would remain an invasion, however minutely fragmented and disposed of, while they remained here.

Impulsively I reached over, swept up the pieces, and stuffed them back inside the Aitken and Drew envelope. I'd introduced the invasion; the least I could do now was remove it. 'I'll find a bin on the way home,' I said, and seeing her nod tucked the envelope in my handbag.

After that, paradoxically, conversation became easier. Not free-flowing – it never was with Joanna – but less formal. I didn't stay long – tea was tea, even at gone seven – but there was time for her to ask about Chris, and, diffidently, marriage (Joanna, perversely, still believed in the institution, though she was careful not to knock the opposition) and I got the chance to ask how the sale of her Norwich house had panned out; her husband had run up so many debts and second mortgages – in her name as well as his – that last winter there had been a danger she wouldn't break even. But she had, she told me, just.

I left at seven-thirty. I hoped, as I walked back to the Holloway Road to hail a taxi, that my visit hadn't ruined Joanna's evening. On balance I suspected it had, but through no fault of mine. If her ex-husband still wrote to her regularly she must have quite a few ruined evenings. And that was down to the tunnel vision of the justice system, and to the fact that her husband had been imprisoned not for what he had done to her, over the years, but for offences that had had no connection with her, or with violence. The victims, if you could call them that, had been the Inland Revenue, Customs and Excise, and her husband's business partner, and the crimes entirely bloodless: embezzlement, fraud and theft.

I forgot about disposing of the torn-up letters until I was in the taxi and halfway home. I thought for a moment and then pulled the glass back and told the driver to pull over at the next litter bin. If he thought me unhinged or criminal the back of his head hid it well; the envelope was disposed of outside a sweet shop in Belsize Park. I had rubbish sacks at home, of course, but they wouldn't leave the flat for days, and I didn't want to be tempted; I'd always had a weakness for jigsaws.

I arrived home feeling relaxed and weightless. Duty done and no loose ends. And serene in the knowledge – unselfish, guiltless knowledge – that unless I was invited I wouldn't be visiting again.

## Chapter 4

From the end of September, when the burglary and my visit to Joanna took place, till Christmas, when I went up to Norwich to stay with my sister's family, three things of personal significance occurred. I got to know Ruth better, and so also Harry, in that I learnt more about their past together; I had my sister's children to stay for their half-term at the end of October; and Chris and I had a terrifying evening out with Ruth and Harry, which ended with Harry lucky not to be arrested for assaulting a police officer.

Less directly involving events during this time included thirteen football fans being killed when a barrier collapsed during a football riot, the savage resumption of street warfare in Lebanon, which left even the commentators at a loss to explain who was killing whom or why, and the cancellation of an East-West arms ratification summit in a fit of blatant gamesmanship on the part of the Americans.

I listened to a Radio Four analysis of the latter: moves, reactions, and counter-moves, and had to turn it off halfway through; not because of what the politicians on both sides were doing (this was pre-Gorbachev, of course, when all negotiations seemed to be conducted at nursery level) but because of the loftily cynical tone of the analyst. Christ, I thought, if even you lot can't take it seriously, if you allow them to go on playing their bloody games with our lives instead of pointing out that all the Emperors are stark naked, what hope for the rest of us? I stomped around the kitchen in a rage, telling my non-existent audience that if creeps like that didn't collude with the madness among people who controlled the fate of the world, and if they had the guts to sound as if they were discussing something of desperate importance, rather than presenting it as a clever-clever piece of journalese that they were making a fat meal-ticket out of, then half the battle would be over. I even composed a letter to this effect in my head, full of references to media flabbiness, indulgence to political posturing, blind deference to sacred cows of 'objectivity' and other needle-sharp acerbities, most of which I had forgotten by the time I finally decided to leave it to someone else to put pen to paper.

When the football tragedy news came through I was downstairs with Ruth, watching the early evening news on the television after an extended coffee and chat session. (No dinky coffee cups or plates of biscuits here – just mugs of Safeway's best and the remains of a packet of Bourbons.) Harry was out, trying to lay his hands on a motorbike part from a contact he'd made through Exchange and Mart. We watched five minutes of edited mayhem and all I could think was: God, what about all the mums and wives at home who don't know yet whether their sons or husbands are safe? The riot had happened only an hour before.

After the clip they wheeled out some politicians and so-called experts for their reactions. The Conservative pundit put it all down to lax discipline in the home (I waited for him to blame working wives but he chickened out), the Labour one blamed unemployment and inner-city deprivation (a year later it would have been Thatcher's children and lager louts) and they both completely ignored a woman from some cumbrously entitled research unit, who made the (to me) sensible and fundamental point that if either of them were wholly right then why weren't there hordes of girls tearing each other limb from limb, since presumably for every ill-disciplined unemployed inner-city boy there must be a female equivalent.

This spurred Ruth to put forward her own brilliantly logical solution – so subversively simple it could never be taken seriously – which was that no male football fan over the height of, say, five foot two, should be admitted to a ground unless accompanied by a woman, child, or pensioner.

We became quite savagely carried away by the ramifications of this, seeing the benefits both for football – encouraging wider interest, and making it a family sport again – and for women, in terms of power (I shan't take you to the match if you don't mow the lawn, wash up dinner, etc., etc.) and employment: queues of women being employed by womanless fans, all strictly controlled by some agency that would get them a decent rate for the job, and screen out the few that were homicidally inclined. In fact once we'd improved the grounds themselves (baby changing facilities, coffee bars, comfortable seats) we couldn't think of any flaws to the system at all, except perhaps initial boredom on the part of women until they got to know other regulars and could treat it as a social outing like any other, and have a good natter about the kids or laugh at the footballers' legs, or possibly even learn the rules of the game and enjoy a little vicarious athleticism.

'Of course,' I ventured, when we'd almost exhausted the subject, 'we may have cracked this, but it's not really getting at the root of the problem, is it?'

'Oh well, if it's roots you want,' said Ruth wearily, 'the only solution's to drown them all at birth.'

Ruth wasn't usually given to making such negative or radical suggestions about men, but on the other hand after what we'd just seen on the television anything else would have seemed too lenient. Anyhow, I justified it as mental revenge for those times I'd been frightened by football fans locally, making their way down to Queen's Park. Mostly kids, and mostly high-spirited rather than aggressive, but still alarming as they crowded and jostled and took over the streets. You couldn't help thinking that if they were just tipped over the edge, or provoked in any way, all that drunken carousing would be transformed in seconds into something much more ugly and dangerous. It might have been only looning about to them, but it wasn't much fun for those of us who had to share the same pavement.

I asked her if Harry liked football. (Chris was moderately interested. He never went to matches, but he watched the big events, Cup Finals, etc., on the television.)

Ruth shook her head definitely. 'Not enough machinery. Cars and motorbikes, they're his thing. He's been to the TT races a few times, and once he went to Le Mans, but he got so drunk he missed the last twelve hours.'

'D'you ever go with him?' I asked.

'Once or twice.' She shrugged. 'Just to see what they're like, really. It's too noisy but the atmosphere's nice. At motorbike events, anyway. It's a very comradely sport. I used to enjoy the rides there. As you get close you link up with crowds of other cyclists. There's lots of banter and excitement.' She smiled, with a trace of embarrassment. 'It sounds silly but it's really quite fun. Although I haven't been for some time, obviously.'

'So Harry's had other bikes while you've known him?'

She nodded vehemently. 'Oh God yes, several. He only got rid of the last one when he left the job at Gatwick to come here. He didn't like it much anyway, and it wasn't really powerful enough for two up. He sold it to a workmate. He's been dying to have the time and space to tackle his dad's old machine.'

This was the first mention of work I'd heard in relation to Harry.

'What did he do at Gatwick?' I asked, intrigued.

'Part of the groundstaff. Turn-around. Making sure the planes are restocked and refuelled before they're off again.' She grinned. 'You should have seen him in his uniform. I mean, it's not a particularly high-powered job but you wouldn't think so from the kit they wear. Airlines are very into status uniforms.'

'Had he worked there long?' What I really wanted to know was how they had first met. For some reason I still felt obliged to skirt around it; perhaps because I didn't trust myself not to betray incredulity at the meeting's success.

'About four years. He liked it. I felt pretty bad about dragging him away, but that's how it goes. It was always understood that I was the one with the career. We did consider living somewhere in-between, but then it seemed silly for both of us to spend hours travelling. Anyway, he's not ambitious for himself. He likes doing what he likes doing . . . it doesn't matter if it's a job or not. If they coincide, like they did at Gatwick – all those great machines to gloat over – fine. But at the moment, well, he's got the break he wanted, and he'll work if he needs the money – for parts for the bike, say – but he's not looking for anything permanent. We can manage on my money, and it's nice for him to be doing something he really enjoys for a while. I mean I am, so why shouldn't he?'

And why not indeed, I thought. Really a very simple, humane philosophy. I reflected on how attitudes had changed. My father, had he been alive, would have described Harry's behaviour as feckless and irresponsible. The idea of a man of his age giving up his own job to follow his partner's profession would have been alien enough to him (especially since Ruth and Harry weren't even married) but then to make no effort to find another, and indeed to choose deliberately to be un-employed in order to tackle a project of his own would have been condemned as behaviour quite as reprehensible as it was incomprehensible.

'In fact he's working next week,' Ruth continued. 'At the young offenders assessment centre in Kensal Rise. He knows the director – he used to be based in Brighton, and Harry did a few stints there some years ago.' She laughed, and possibly my expression prompted her to add, 'Not as an offender, you understand. He did projects with the boys, motor mechanics usually. He's really good with them, especially the younger ones. The director would like him to come in permanently, but he won't, not yet, anyway. Says a month will suit him fine. Just long enough to pay for bits for the bike and give him some pocket money for Christmas, and finish servicing all the staff's cars, which is what he normally gets the boys doing.'

I said, 'Good heavens,' but mostly because I was surprised that there was such an institution locally. Kensal Rise was less than ten minutes' walk from the flats, and I'd never heard of it. I could actually imagine Harry being rather good with teenage boys. At least he'd hardly get written off as a do-gooding wimp. Indeed, I thought, recalling my own first impressions of him, he was probably just the sort of man they would have absolutely no difficulty identifying with.

On that occasion I still didn't discover how Ruth and Harry had met. I'm not sure why I was so keen to find out; I wouldn't have described myself, normally, as an excessively nosy person. But perhaps it was because they hadn't become any more alike in the weeks I'd known them, and at the back of my mind I thought learning about it might provide some clue to their relationship.

And in a way I was right; the way their lives had collided did tell me something about the people they were. After Harry's brush with the law in November Ruth told me about it, among other things, while she was having a despairing moan about his capacity to mastermind his own misfortunes.

What had happened, she told me, was that Harry had got a previous girlfriend pregnant. This was years back: Harry had been twenty-two, and the girl only eighteen, about to go off to college. The girl still lived at home and her parents, who didn't like Harry anyway, had been furious about it and had packed her off to relatives, after first pressurizing her to agree to an abortion. But before she had it Harry had tracked her down and tried to persuade her to have the baby, with some wild idea about looking after it himself, so she could still go to college. The girl hadn't been sufficiently determined to give him no hope, and indeed in the few minutes before he was forcibly ejected from the house even promised to delay the abortion until he could sort out his rights as father; and that was where Ruth had come in. Of course he had no rights at all, since they weren't married (and apparently wouldn't have had many if they had been). However, he refused to give up, and approached the girl again, this time in an attempt to persuade her to have the baby and put it up for adoption, with a view to adopting it himself. He didn't stand a chance here either, as a single young man, but he caused enough fuss to alarm the parents into taking a court order out against him, although as Ruth said, if they'd only had the sense to let their daughter and Harry meet calmly and thrash it out between them, without bullying her or baying for his blood, the whole matter could have been sorted out in hours and needn't have involved the law or nearly so much bad feeling on both sides. Ruth was almost sure the girl genuinely didn't want the baby and would have had the abortion anyway. If she had just been allowed to say that to Harry and make it clear that it was her decision and not her parents', a lot of grief could have been avoided. Although if Harry had behaved more responsibly in the first place, or made the slightest effort to endear himself to the parents before he got their daughter pregnant, the same would have been equally true. Ruth described it as a typical Harry cock-up, with him not exactly to blame but not altogether innocent, either.

That was when I first learnt that Harry wanted children. From the way Ruth told it, it was definitely only the baby he was desperate not to lose, not the girl. She said he had haunted her office for weeks with ever more outlandish schemes to save the child, and didn't give up until he got the news that the deed was done, which, with solicitors now involved on both sides, she had to break to him herself. She'd taken him out for a drink to console him, and this had somehow ended up with Harry comatose at her flat, and the start of their own affair.

She sounded almost sad when she described her feelings for him then. (I should say that these confidences were unexpected and, for Ruth, out of character, but she made them only two days after our terrible evening out together, and indirectly, I suspect, they were by way of an apology.)

'I'd never met such an extraordinary person,' she said. 'He got incapably drunk, passed out cold, and then that was that. No vindictiveness, no self-pity, nothing. Just picked himself up and started again. And he was so different from anyone I'd had a relationship with before. To begin with I honestly didn't think it could last, but, well . . . it was so easy. He's never tried to change me. I'm afraid I did try to change him at first – not consciously, perhaps, but because of the kind of relationships I'd had before, where you sort of mould yourself around each other. But then I realized what I was doing and that it was causing problems, so I stopped. Life is so straightforward with Harry. He gets on with his life, and lets me get on with mine. And he's totally reliable. If he says he'll do something, he does it, and it never gets flung back at me. If he doesn't want to, he'll say so, and probably won't do it. But at least I always know exactly where I stand.'

I made no comment. Because I guessed the confidences were forced by circumstance, I thought Ruth might regret them later, and I didn't want to encourage her. However, she went on anyway:

'And although he wants kids, he doesn't go on about it. I told him I'd think about it – I'm not giving up work and if we did he'd have to look after them – and he hasn't bullied me about it, because he trusts me not to have forgotten. And I haven't, but I haven't made up my mind either.' She sighed. 'It's the one thing I feel bad about. I tell myself it was his choice to live with me and he knew what I was like then, but it doesn't really help. The trouble is I'm happy now, and I don't want anything to change. If we had children I'd love them, and worry about them, whoever was actually staying at home to look after them, and there would still be all that endless responsibility. I don't want to be a cosy domestic unit, welded by kids, always knowing exactly where the other one is, and whose turn it is to take them swimming, and all the claustrophobia that brings. I don't want to get bored with him, nor him with me. Friends can have good honest rows, but that endless bickering and contempt you see in couples . . . And it's all because they see too much of each other and have to depend on each other too much, and that's because of the kids.'

She shrugged unhappily. 'I suppose I'm being selfish. But you shouldn't have children unless you really want them, and I honestly don't think I do. And Harry's no use. He can't explain why he wants them.' She smiled, as if imagining

Harry giving a lucid explanation of anything was a faintly ridiculous idea. 'He'll only say that he likes them, and he'd do everything for them if we had them.' She shook her head. 'But it isn't as simple as that. He doesn't understand how it would alter us. And while it might change him for the better in some ways – make him less introverted, perhaps, and give him something to grow up for – that can't be a good enough reason to have children. Not when you think what it involves. And yet sometimes . . . sometimes I think, yes, it would be a big adventure, and it would make him happy, and everybody else does, and they must do it for some reason . . .' She glanced at me apologetically, suddenly aware that not everybody else does, but not too apologetically, because she was one childless woman talking to another, and added, 'But then I think, no, don't spoil what you've got, don't go into it when you know it's a bottomless pit, waiting to swallow you up. I don't want to stop being me, as I am now, and I would, whatever Harry says, if I had children. I couldn't carry on as if they were nothing to do with me. It's unrealistic. He doesn't think ahead. He simply knows what he wants, and wants it, without stopping to think what it would mean. But I can't do that. Perhaps that's the main difference between us.'

I doubted this at the time, since I could think of a multitude of other differences, most of them much more openly apparent. But later I realized she was right. Ruth is a worker-out. She's an assembler of facts, reviewer of alternatives, and calculator of consequences. She's got that sort of mind, and it's what she's good at. Of course she has feelings too, but she doesn't trust them on their own; they have to be justified and explained, rationalized into validity. Lots of people are like that, men especially, and I don't think any the less of them for it.

But Harry wasn't like that. He didn't bother to work anything out, mostly because he trusted his instincts and therefore didn't need to, but also because he couldn't see the point. A fundamental disregard of long-term perspectives – including the consequences of his own actions – was one of his hallmarks, perhaps because he was fatalistic enough to accept what life dished out, and didn't have too much faith in his power to change things significantly. He reacted to the here-and-now, which was within his grasp, and let the future look after itself, and that attitude, I'm sure, determined much more of his behaviour than anything wilfully negative. As far as people were concerned, he reckoned that if they were going to like him they were going to like him; if they weren't they weren't and that was that. He certainly didn't see it as anything he had a duty to work on.

And there was absolutely no need for him to work on it with children. When Jamie and Zoe came down at half-term they took to him immediately, even though he didn't appear to do anything to ingratiate himself with them, unlike some adults (more to impress the parents, I've always thought, than out of any great love of children). In fact he told Jamie he'd get a thumping if he mucked about with the bike frame outside (the mechanical bits were by now stored away upstairs) and luckily as soon as Jamie realized it wasn't going anywhere, and wasn't even capable of noise, he lost interest. Zoe, once over her initial shyness, became his adoring slave.

His talent with children was not, I think, because they recognized any kindred spirit in him, even though children too are renowned for their lack of foresight, so that superficially at least that quality was held in common. But young humans are like that because they are immature and inexperienced, not because they have abandoned such speculations as pointless.

They are not fatalistic, and indeed we should probably be very worried if they were; it's my experience that they have an infinite faith in their power, or the power of their guardians, to adapt the world to their taste, and some lucky individuals even seem to retain this capacity into their adult lives, as idealism and enthusiasm, rather than disappointing it into cynicism or fatalism. And Harry was not childlike in any other way; but they still adored him.

We took the children out – or rather they accompanied us out – for a drink to a pub with a large beer garden, as the weather was so unseasonably mild, and when he wasn't fighting with Jamie, Zoe was mauling him around atrociously in her usual tactile way, an ordeal he endured with commendable patience, and from which he could only distract her long enough to have a few swigs of beer himself by sending her off on countless small and useless errands, such as picking up crisp packets, or fetching beer mats, or calculating exactly how many footsteps wide and long the garden was. The children looked like lunatics as they teetered back and forth, mouthing numbers with intense concentration, but it gave Harry five minutes of respite before Zoe returned to fling herself over him again.

Watching her, I thought what a good thing it was that my brother-in-law Brian wasn't there. He hated it when she performed her octopus act with men (apart from himself, of course). It made him uncomfortable, as if he believed there was something knowing and seductive about it. Berry and I had often pointed out that the fact that it conjured up more self-conscious adult behaviour must be more a reflection on grown-up sexual activity than children's, given the chronology. Or maybe it was just an expression of something natural and universal, at any age. We're the same species, after all. I can still remember specific emotions and fears I experienced at seven

(Zoe's age then; Jamie was eight), and can vividly recall my first day at school, when the feelings weren't so different from my first day teaching at college; except that I wasn't wearing a felt hat with elastic that I managed to ping in my eyes as I struggled to take it off, which made me look as if I was crying, and I certainly didn't sit on anyone's knee for the enrolment session because of it. But I would have definitely welcomed some of the same motherly affection as I wandered round the place in a daze, wondering if I'd ever get to know all these strange people, or work out how to get back to the main lobby after I'd become hopelessly lost in the endless and identical corridors.

So the children's stay with me was even more of a success than it usually was. This half-term arrangement, I should explain, had something of a contrived logic to it. I didn't have a half-term holiday any more than Brian or Berry (he works for the planning department of the local authority, she for the DSS) but my college ran crêches at half-terms for all those lecturers and other employees who had children, staffed by students taking nursery nurse courses and the like. And because Jamie and Zoe stayed with me regularly they knew lots of other children, so going to the crêche was a great treat for them, like a permanent kids' party, with dozens of old friends to meet up with, and all in the enterprising care of a very tolerant and freshly enthusiastic team of workers. It was a satisfactory arrangement all round: Brian and Berry paid the charges, and reckoned it worth every penny, and I got the chance to play temporary mother, but without having to do it twenty-four hours a day.

On my afternoons off I usually took them with a friend and her children to one of the big museums to have a simulated earthquake, or practise being in the womb; or if I was feeling especially strong, to be ignobled by dinosaurs, of which Jamie knew all the unpronounceable names. I'm afraid dinosaurs, and the crowds around them, left me frazzled. And how should I know which would win, if a Stegosaurus fought with a Triceratops? I usually said something like 'Neither, they were both eaten by a Tyrannosaurus Rex,' which was my adult way of wriggling out of a sticky situation. Jamie was scornful of ignorance among grown-ups. His patronizing tone, and the way he punctuated every pronouncement with 'don't you know, stupid . . .' was eventually wearing, though in other respects he was turning into quite a nice boy. His energy was colossal. At the crèche he spent the entire day wrestling with other small boys under the ping-pong table, emerging late afternoon scarlet in the face but happy as a sand-boy, and still had enough get-up-and-go to loon around the flat all evening and refuse to go to bed till nine o'clock.

But he had at least reached the stage where if you could persuade him to stand still long enough to hold a conversation, he could actually see your point of view, and make perceptive remarks about what other people might think, or what their motives might be. While Zoe, although she was a much more restful child and much more anxious to please, was still at the age where she didn't honestly think of anyone beyond herself, and worried about how much she was liked (hence the ingratiating co-operation) and who her best friend was going to be when she got home, because they'd all have been seeing each other, and she might get left out, and it wasn't fair. She was more insecure than Jamie in lots of ways, but a delicious child to cuddle, very melting and relaxed (unlike Jamie, who had all the sensual properties of a conger eel) so I gave her plenty of love and affection while she was here.

★

On this occasion it was Brian's turn to collect the children at the end of the half-term and the handover took place, as usual, in Liverpool Street station buffet.

We arrived to find Brian already there in a corner seat, deep in the *Observer* colour supplement. He was wearing one of his Michelin Man ski-jacket monstrosities, and, seated beside a sari-clad Asian lady, looked huge and overdressed.

As usual I was touched – and, maybe presumptuously, reassured – by the uninhibited warmth with which he greeted his children. He leaped to his feet and swept them up in a babbling bundle of arms and legs. It was one of Berry's gripes that he was always more demonstrative towards them in public than in private (implying I'm not sure what) but, true or otherwise, there was no doubting the sincerity of the gesture.

He planted a kiss on me, too, which I returned with genuine but slightly reserved affection. Brian, to me, is like Christmas; a pleasure in distant anticipation and in retrospect, but surprisingly stressful in-between. This meeting, brief though it was, was no exception. We had time for a cup of coffee before their train returned to Norwich and we'd hardly sat down and stabbed our way into the sterilized milk sachets than we were edging metaphorical knives towards each other. The precipitating subject was, predictably, my love life.

Brian had already established in the coffee queue that the children had behaved themselves over the week and that no catastrophes had occurred. Now he leant towards me over the table and said, 'Well? How's our Chris keeping?'

This sounds an entirely reasonable enquiry, especially given that Brian and Chris were good friends; however, Brian's delivery – imbued with undertones of reproach and weary pessimism – rendered it nothing of the sort. In my ears he was clearly saying: and how's that decent man you're playing with, sweetie – still stringing him along?

I jabbed a plastic straw into Jamie's fruit juice carton and replied curtly, 'Fine, as far as I'm aware.'

Brian looked nonplussed. His preconceptions about me are so deeply entrenched he simply can't hear them echoed in his speech.

'Only asked,' he said, sounding aggrieved.

'OK,' I said, neutrally. 'And I've answered.'

He gave me one of his God-women-are-difficult looks and said testily, 'What's it with you? I am allowed to ask, aren't I?'

'Of course,' I said. And in a more conciliatory tone – sparring with him wasn't worth it; I never learnt – 'Really, he's fine. We're both fine.'

'Good,' he said emphatically. He drew Zoe on to his lap, said, 'Ah ah,' as she tried to cram her thumb into her mouth, and then in the child's ear but with his eyes on me, he muttered with mock resignation, 'I dunno, eh, I dunno.'

I don't learn. I'd have sprung in again if we'd had more time. To pursue what, precisely, he thought he didn't know – and to prove that in fact he meant the opposite. But I swallowed my irritation.

The exchange, though, was typical of our relationship. That is, difficult altogether: layers of familiarity and affection laid down over the years, shot through with liberal seams of mistrust and disapproval on his side, and needles of retaliatory aggression on mine. The disapproval related to my persistently single status – he's one of those who can't understand a woman choosing to live her life alone, and thinks there has to be something suspect in it – and the mistrust was linked to this, but was mainly a hangover from the past, a perverse vestige of the days when he couldn't trust himself with me.

This was rooted in an actual incident in our youth. Once, at a drunken party – long before he and Berry were married – he became recklessly carried away, and made a determined attempt to get me into bed with him. And if he hadn't been attached to my sister, so to speak, I very likely would have gone. He hasn't aged very well, and at thirty-five already had a noticeable belly and had become rather jowelly, but at twenty he was a muscular young man with an ego of irresistible proportions, and I can't deny I felt attracted to him. (Which he knew, of course, as he confided so persuasively while trying to take advantage of it.)

And although nothing actually happened he subsequently managed – with archetypal male logic – to transpose this minor transgression in his mind so that he could blame me for the lust he once felt towards me, of which he was now ashamed. This meant that while I remained a free spirit and theoretically available, he couldn't quite trust me.

He would also claim I gave Berry ideas, blithely over-looking the fact that Berry had plenty of ideas of her own, what with her active involvement in the women's movement and campaigns for this and that. But he hadn't, as yet, caught up with that side of her life, and hadn't seen that her association with women was much more undermining of their marriage than if she were out seeing men. Despite calling himself a left-winger (though a more materialistic socialist would be hard to find) he remained remarkably innocent as far as women's politics were concerned.

Luckily for him Berry appeared to have given him up as a lost cause. She seemed to have decided that it wasn't his fault she'd turned into someone else along the way, and that she therefore had a duty to compromise her principles where he was concerned. Not that she had to compromise them very far: he's a decent man, at heart, and a competent father. Besides, he isn't one to look for trouble: any annoyance he might have felt at Berry's lack of enthusiasm in delivering her end of the marital bargain was hinted at in tone of voice and turn of phrase, not in a form he couldn't wriggle out of if directly challenged. As in, for instance, his attitude to these half-term arrangements over the children. He always thanked me effusively – as he did on this occasion, while shepherding the children on to the platform – suggesting that it was some enormous chore I had been railroaded into; and went on to make the usual point of saying how lucky Berry was, as if she had been let off a hook she should rightfully have been impaled upon, as a duty of motherhood.

Though possibly it was a complicated way of distancing me too; I had, after all, no right to his children, even if they were important to me. But being a good aunt is easy, compared to being a good mother – or a good father, for that matter – and perhaps Brian, in his own oblique way, was not above reminding me of that.

# Chapter 5

The night Harry got into trouble was a cinema trip. It was also the first night that Chris and I went out as a couple with Ruth and Harry, and the whole evening was pretty much a disaster.

When Chris and I called at the bottom flat to collect the others only Ruth was there. I introduced Chris and could tell instantly that they were going to get along. Indeed, within minutes they were both poring over her leather-bound copy of Mrs Gaskell's *Ruth* – Chris always looked at bookshelves and had immediately spotted it. Ruth said her godmother had bought it for her from an antique book stall without realizing that it was about the redemption of fallen women. We sat chatting in their sitting room a while longer and then when I glanced at my watch Ruth leapt to her feet and said she'd better go and fetch Harry who, it turned out, was still tinkering with the bike engine upstairs.

She came back down with him and he nodded and said, 'Hello,' briefly to Chris.

Chris nodded back, equally briefly. I thought God, now we've all got to hang about while Harry gets cleaned up and changed, knowing how long it took Chris to get organized to go out anywhere. Whoever said that women spend ages getting themselves ready was certainly a man. Chris never stepped into a shower until I was putting my coat on, and Brian always waited until Berry arrived breathless with two bladder-emptied and becoated children before deciding he must check the tyres or the brake fluid on the car, when everything could have been done hours before if he hadn't been reading *Private Eye* in the toilet all morning.

But in fact all Harry did was wash his hands and put on his leather jacket – his jeans weren't excessively oily, though he did make the rest of us look marginally overdressed – and then we strolled down The Avenue towards Willesden Lane to catch the bus. This had been my idea; Chris had his car and could have driven us, but he was an appalling driver (hesitant and aggressive, a lethal combination) and anyway – my ostensible argument – parking near the cinema was imposs-ible.

Chris, Ruth and I walked abreast, chatting among our-selves, while Harry trailed unsociably some way behind. It amazed me that Ruth let him get away with it. She didn't act as if she had any allegiance or responsibility towards him at all.

We arrived at the bus stop and then, infuriatingly, the bus wouldn't come. Normally they were every ten minutes or so, more often in the rush hour, and I'd never had difficulties with them before, but it's typical that when a bus knows you have been its personal advocate it should suddenly become shy and retiring, and refuse to put in an appearance.

Our attitudes to the wait were very different. Ruth didn't appear to notice how long we were there; the minor frustra-tion rather seemed to bring out the humorist in her. She devised a fantasy picture of queues of buses hiding in the darkness round the corner, red and malicious, waiting for us to give up so they could stream past in convoy, just as we were far enough from the bus stop to make a dash back impractical.

I like that sense of the ridiculous, and I wouldn't have minded the wait so much if I hadn't felt so responsible for it. Chris became irritable because he was convinced we were going to miss the beginning of the film, and it was one he particularly wanted to see. He kept suggesting we go back and fetch the car, and we kept saying, 'No no, it's not worth it, it's bound to come any minute,' except it didn't, and in the time we waited we could have fetched a dozen cars. Harry spent the time casing the neighbourhood like a diligent burglar, ambling up and down staring at the houses. Occasionally he would lean against a lamp-post, or sit on someone's garden wall, before restlessness overcame him again and he was off for another perambulation. He reminded me of Jamie, slowed down several hundred miles an hour.

Eventually a bus did appear, and then Chris embarrassed me by saying snidely to the driver as he paid his fare, 'Ever thought of joining British Rail?' I did sympathize, but felt he ought to have made the effort to keep the atmosphere good-humoured. I wasn't like Ruth; I couldn't help feeling that the behaviour of my partner did reflect on me, and so wanted other people to like them, and felt impelled to assist that liking. I just prayed that the rest of the evening went smoothly: once Chris got annoyed every trivial inconvenience became a major catastrophe. If we'd been alone I'd have told him not to get so worked up about something he could do nothing about, but as it was I found myself making brightly encouraging remarks to jolly him out of his ill-humour, a demeaning exercise that only made me irritable too.

We saw the film (except the first five minutes – Chris was right) and when we emerged, with that strange sort of silence peculiar to adults, nobody wanting to be the one to comment first (unlike with children – 'Which was your best bit? . . . I liked the monster chase . . . did the actor mind having his hand cut off ?') the pub we went into was stiflingly crowded, and I hate drinking standing up. By this time I had a slight headache, and all I wanted to do was go home and draw a veil over the evening. But even when we agreed not to bother with another round we still had the return journey ahead of us. This time we decided to give the bus ten minutes and if it failed to appear get a taxi – give it something to compete with, as Ruth said.

When we arrived at the bus stop it looked as if the threat had worked, because there were other people waiting, which meant we couldn't have just missed one. We grouped ourselves against a low wall at the side of the pavement to talk; and that was when the trouble started.

From the direction of the cinema four boys with very short hair and boots approached – genuine boys; none of them looked old enough to drink legally in a pub – and as they passed between us and the bus queue one of them said, 'Fucking wankers!' very loudly, unmistakably at us.

None of us said anything in reply. I was more surprised than annoyed; it seemed such an unprovoked fit of childishness.

But Harry, sitting on the wall behind us, couldn't resist lifting his fingers to their retreating faces – they were walking away backwards, laughing and jostling, as if there was nothing they liked better than insulting complete strangers.

And at this the boys stopped, with mock-outraged expressions on their faces, looked at each other and slowly came back.

Ruth immediately moved between Harry and the boys and turned her back on them. Chris and I stood transfixed, wondering what the hell was going to happen next.

It was just talk to begin with, aimed at Harry.

'That wasn't a very polite thing to do, was it, shithead?' said one, a blond boy, giving a nasty sideways smile to Chris and myself. A ringleader's smirk, I thought. His hair was so short you could see his scalp through it.

'D'you always hide behind your tart, then?' said his mate, bobbing up and down to see over Ruth's shoulder.

'Course he does,' another nodded wisely. He spat on the pavement. 'Fucking wanker.'

Harry did nothing, merely looked at Ruth (though not without a hint of dog waiting to be let off leash) and she stayed exactly where she had positioned herself, facing him and with her back to the boys, cutting off face-to-face contact between them.

But then, because there were four of them, and they all wanted to show how brave and tough they were, and without moving Ruth they couldn't even see their quarry properly, much less get at him, two of them – the blond boy and his mate – turned their attention to Chris.

'You ought to teach your friend some manners,' the blond boy suggested. His pale blue eyes looked alarmingly as if there was nothing behind them.

'If you move the tarts out the way we'd be glad to do it for you,' his friend added helpfully, and they both laughed.

I wished I had a camera: I'm sure the boys thought they looked macho and swaggering, but they didn't. They looked out of control, hopped up – they jiggled around constantly, like children desperate to use the lavatory – and quite repellent. I tried telling myself that they were all unemployed with drunken fathers and absentee mothers, but I still wanted to stamp on them and grind their horrible screwed-up faces into the dirt.

A number of lewd suggestions and insults followed. Their vocabulary was tediously limited, even in its range of obscenities. Wankers and tarts figured heavily. I was tempted to snap back that, since Harry and Chris were the ones out with women, it was much more likely that they themselves were the wankers, but managed to restrain myself. Instead I did the same as Ruth and placed myself in front of Chris; but as he was standing, and was a lot taller than I am, it didn't have the same effect, and they could still talk directly to his face and see his reactions.

And then he had to say, 'Oh shove off, can't you,' which was mild enough, under the circumstances, but still too much.

'Got another one here,' the boys crowed.

'Doesn't anyone teach them manners any more?' I heard back, followed by a high-pitched, over-excited giggle.

The two baiting Chris started dancing up and down behind me, issuing a torrent of crudely vicious remarks. I started to feel frightened. Although Chris was tall he wasn't athletically built, and I was sure he'd never had a fight in his adult life. He had gone very white, and whilst he seemed to be coping reasonably well with insults directed at himself I could sense he was having difficulty when they made references to me and Ruth, as if he felt he ought to be defending our honour at least. And the people at the bus queue were doing absolutely nothing, except staring fixedly away from us, determinedly ignoring the incident.

I didn't see the first blow. One of the boys behind me had just made a horrible remark about me (to be accurate, a specific part of me) and Chris looked away and muttered, 'Jesus,' between his teeth. That's all it took. I heard a voice say, 'Don't turn away when I'm talking to you, cunt,' and something – an arm – whistled past my shoulder. Chris swore and put a hand to his nose, and blood began to pour through his fingers.

From then the sequence of events became confused, because the sight of blood seemed to excite the boys into a frenzy of abuse and leaping about. The next thing that registered was when one of them – probably in an unsuccessful attempt to get at Chris again – punched me on the shoulder blade; not in fact painfully, but sharply enough to knock me forward and force me to turn round and face them.

At that point Harry must have decided that matters had gone far enough, or perhaps Ruth did, because she made no attempt to stop him. He was suddenly in front of me, grabbed one of the lads – the blond one, I was glad to see – pushed him backwards at speed and tipped him on to the pavement. It wasn't much of a contest, one to one like that. The lad was resisting furiously but Harry was much bigger and stronger and had momentum and balance on his side; it actually looked quite easy.

So much for solidarity among thugs; the moment Harry intervened the others were off. All four of them could surely have dealt with him – him and Chris, for that matter – but somehow once they had lost the initiative all that bravado evaporated. The three of them galloped off down the road – whooping and shouting, as if it were victory rather than rout they were celebrating – and Harry sat down on the one he had got and delivered a number of swift punches into the boy's back.

At that moment, with a squeal of brakes and the machine-gun rattle of a tyre-rocked drain-cover, a policecar swept up.

No one had called them, I'm sure, they were just a routine patrol, but they couldn't have chosen more unfortunate timing.

Two officers leapt out of the car and pounded across the pavement. They hoiked Harry to his feet – ignoring the fact that he was getting up anyway – and, twisting one arm behind his back, started to manhandle him vigorously towards the car.

The boy Harry'd been sitting on jumped to his feet and hared off down the road. The police shouted 'Oi!' after him, but couldn't stop him: Harry was trying to explain what had happened, and insisting on trying to do it without being pushed around, and it was taking both officers to get him slammed up against the policecar.

Ruth moaned, 'Oh Jesus,' and tore over to explain as well, and to persuade them to stop trying to break Harry's arm. Chris was still immobilized beside me, trying to stem the unabated flow from his nose with his handkerchief.

The trouble with Harry was that he didn't treat policemen with respect. He treated them as ordinary men like himself, who could take being called 'ignorant cretins' and 'fucking idiots' or worse (as indeed he had just proved). Or perhaps, taking a broader view, he recognized in them an agency that was capable of doing him a lot of harm, and which was therefore worthy of the hostility such threat demanded. He wasn't actually fighting them – he wasn't in a position to, with his chest banged up against the car – but he was unco-operative and insolent, and making them very cross.

Ruth was crying, 'For Christ's sake, we were the ones who were attacked, he was only trying to protect us.' And 'For God's sake, let him go, you're hurting him' – which they were, too: we couldn't see his face but every time they jerked his arm up his head snapped back, and they were banging him pretty hard against the policecar. But she was appealing to preoccupied ears. They kept telling her to move out of the way, as if they'd got a dangerous criminal barely subdued, or she too might be in danger. They may not even have grasped that Harry was with us. He had been a short distance away when they pounced on him, and may not have looked like someone they would associate with our party.

In the end, since they couldn't get him to stand still against the car by hurting him, they wrenched his other arm back too, produced a small metallic object, and handcuffed him.

I was deeply shocked; I'd never seen anyone handcuffed in real life before, only on celluloid, when it is so sanitized and routine you don't stop to think what it means, or how acutely uncomfortable it is to witness. I could scarcely bear to watch.

When they swung Harry round we could see his lip was bleeding, but of course there was nothing he could do about it.

Ruth, tight-faced with anger, tried to use her handkerchief on him, but the officers wouldn't let her. One of them slapped Harry's legs apart and started patting him up and down in the most bizarre manner: it took me a moment to grasp he was performing a body search.

Harry, to my astonished relief, looked quite unhumiliated by this treatment. He rolled his eyes in our direction, as if to say 'what ignorant morons this lot are'.

Ruth looked agonized; she frowned at him urgently and turned with a despairing shrug to the officer beside her.

'Where are you taking him?' she asked.

'All in good time, miss.' He didn't look at her; he was watching the search.

'Take their numbers!' Harry called.

At this the officer doing the search broke off and pushed his face close to Harry's ear. His lips said something, inaudible to the rest of us but short and emphatic. Harry stared back at him with contempt. The officer took a step backwards and flicked a violent hand at the front of Harry's jacket. For a terrible moment I thought it was a blow. Ruth scrabbled frantically in her handbag for a pen.

One of the officers pulled Harry away from the car and the other opened the back door.

'Careful,' Ruth moaned as they started to bundle him through, and then, 'Oh Christ,' as his head struck the car roof.

'He's OK,' the policeman said, and slammed the door shut. Then, with Harry safely contained and silenced, one got out his radio and the other walked over to us and started asking us what had happened.

From that moment the policemen became recognizable as ordinary bobbies; for the first time I noticed what they looked like as men, rather than as aggressively animated uniforms: our questioner was middle-aged, moustached, and almost avuncular now in manner, and the other – the one who had done most of the arm-wrenching, and performed the search – was the over-eager schoolboy type, his face against the radio deeply action-flushed.

Everybody in the bus queue gave their versions, as did we, several times, while the officer took careful notes. So also, hovering behind him, did Ruth.

'May I ask what you're doing?' the officer enquired, turning from examining Chris's nose to see her scribbling.

'I'm the solicitor for the man you've got in the car,' she said, continuing to write.

The officer looked sceptical, till she produced a business card to prove it. He motioned for her to accompany him to his partner, and the three of them went into a huddle by the car. It looked as if an argument was going on.

She returned to us a moment later. 'I'm sorry,' she said distractedly, 'I've got to get a taxi. They won't let me go with him.' She looked back at the policecar. The officers were shutting themselves inside. 'I think it'll be all right. They're just a bit bolshie at the moment.' She gazed at the car intensely, then turned abruptly away. 'Damn Harry,' she said violently. 'If they touch him, I'll bloody kill them.'

(Afterwards, she told me that this was what she was really afraid of. Something similar had happened in Brighton. That time, Harry had been picked up on a freezing February night for loitering suspiciously outside the Royal Sussex Hospital, while waiting for Ruth to finish visiting a girlfriend. The officers said they were going to book him but instead drove him to the silent cliff-top grounds of Roedean School and rolled him in the dirt for his insolence. Ruth had been frantic for hours, because Harry had then made his way down to the undercliff walk and attempted to clean himself up in the icy sea. Luckily he was found before he froze to death by a middle-aged couple out walking their dog by torchlight, who bravely led him back to the coast road and then ruined the interior of their car by driving him the couple of miles back to Ruth's flat. Ruth said she had briefly considered giving up the law, and Harry, in her fury at both.)

But the policecar disappeared, as did Ruth, in anxious pursuit, and Chris and I were left shaking and disoriented to muddle our way home on the bus. We should have got a taxi too, but the bus arrived almost immediately and we automatically climbed aboard.

All the other passengers were naturally fascinated by the sight of Chris's swollen and bloody nose. I couldn't think of a thing to say to him in such a public place, so we didn't speak for the entire journey, and nothing of much significance was said on the short walk back to the flat. He was intending to spend the night with me anyway, so there was no question of having to persuade him not to drive home. In the mood he was in he would probably have mown down half London, just for the hell of it. But it was a very quiet, private kind of fury, and I knew he wasn't going to share it with me. I felt achingly sorry for him. I couldn't know exactly what he was suffering, because it wasn't me who was punched on the nose, and I'm not a man, and I don't know what it must feel like to watch another man hammer the person who has humiliated me and insulted my girlfriend. But I could see that whatever else it felt like, it was acutely painful, and included a lot of anger, and that some of that anger was directed at Harry.

I wanted to say, 'I don't like violent men, and you did nothing wrong, and if Harry was stupid enough to start it then perhaps it was up to him to stop it, and nobody's keeping scores'; but I didn't say it, and I knew, because I could feel it myself, that somehow Harry had come out of it better than Chris, even if he was now banged up in a police cell somewhere. And I knew too that whatever Harry was suffering, unless the police were actually taking him apart, it was nothing compared to Chris's anguish. When we went to bed he was mutely rigid in my arms for hours, and for the first time ever we spent a night together without even thinking about making love.

## Chapter 6

They didn't charge Harry with anything, or harm a hair on his head, and the next morning he was off to work with a swollen lip and an unchastened air (I saw him leave as I was drawing the sitting-room curtains before preparing a pampering breakfast for Chris) and doubtless the young offenders were most impressed.

Chris and I never properly discussed the incident, though perhaps we should have; but we had to go to work, and his nose returned to normal, and time kind of slipped away, and after that I didn't like to raise the subject myself, since he seemed to want to forget about it.

And November faded to December, and Harry gave up his job, and a bomb went off in Oxford Street to herald the start of the Christmas rush.

Three people were killed: a child, a woman and a policeman who was trying to clear the area before the warning expired. We'd had a bomb scare at work once, years before. Although everybody had known it must be a hoax, and was almost certainly one of the students wreaking an obscure revenge, or playing a tasteless joke, it was still a heart-stopping experience. One of the porters toured the rooms telling us all to gather in the carpark because there was a bomb in the building – he made it sound as if he'd seen it personally – and my mind went a complete and static-filled blank. All I overwhelmingly wanted to do was get out, as quickly as possible. I didn't give a thought to anyone else – I wasn't with students at the time – and I was even stupid enough to use the lift, because I thought the stairs would be just the place to leave a bomb to inflict maximum carnage as everyone fled the building. After the chaos of that occasion the college instituted proper drills, for fire, bombs, plague, anything, but of course it never happened again.

After the Oxford Street atrocity I was outraged, like everyone else, but not personally frightened. I rarely shopped in Oxford Street and never at Christmas, because of the crowds. In fact organized shopping scarcely figured in my schedule at all, because I disliked it so much. Especially clothes shopping; I considered myself, for a thirtysomething, a fairly reasonable shape, and quite liked what I saw in the mirror at home, clothed or unclothed. But on the journey between home and the changing rooms of shops I gained at least a stone, my body flesh became pale and pimply, and a disheartening latticework of lines and flaky patches appeared all over my face. Not that it's ever been my best feature; I was always a little disappointed when I concentrated on that area in the mirror, even at home, because I felt prettier than the rather ordinary-looking woman staring back, with the slightly lumpy nose and noticeably crooked teeth, though her complexion was pleasingly reliable, and only let me down if I was exceptionally overtired.

Berry once said generously that I shouldn't worry about how I looked in mirrors or photographs, because it was movement that made my face attractive. And I can vouch for the fact that it made me look different, at least. The first time we did a video workshop at college it took me several seconds to realize which was me; once I recognized myself my brain became too dizzy for rational judgements, but in those first innocent moments I had definitely labelled that animated-looking stranger with long hair and a middle-class voice as attractive, so perhaps she was right.

This became a pitiable delusion, however, after a session in changing rooms. In fact the only expeditions I positively enjoyed were to bookshops, or toyshops, so at Christmas most adults received books as presents, and I always spent more than I intended on Jamie and Zoe. Though not excessively so, as Brian and Berry weren't the type to give their children outrageously expensive presents (even if all their classmates were getting computers and brand-new bicycles) and it wouldn't have done for me to give them something grander than their parents.

I tended to buy them lots of silly things and a couple of paperbacks each that could go unattributed into their stockings, and then something they had particularly asked for, gleaned via Berry. That Christmas it was a rucksack and water bottle for Jamie (who was going to be a naturalist when he grew up, and discover a land where dinosaurs still roamed) and reluctantly, but on the principle that adults shouldn't always know best, a Sindy horse for Zoe, who still revelled in the fripperies of rampant femininity, despite Berry's best efforts.

I ingeniously stashed all the other presents in the rucksack for the train journey to Norwich, and must have looked a most unlikely hiker, with that on my back over my Next catalogue wool jacket, and my smart leather case in my hand.

Chris spent the holiday with his parents and then escaped as soon as decency allowed to join us all in Norwich. It's my favourite city, Norwich: big enough to produce the electricity of a city, and have all the advantages of a city (such as proper bookshops) yet small enough to walk across, knowing you are still breathing country air, and that somehow, despite the electricity, the ratrace has blissfully passed it by. I don't like rural Norfolk much; the fields are too big, there aren't enough hedges, and a lot of it looks sterile, but the Broads are still Arthur Ransome territory, there are fossils on the endless beaches, and the sky is magnificent.

As usual we crammed in as much dissipation as we could handle, and some of us were out each night, Berry and I with a crowd of her women friends at the Labour Club (plotting their overthrow, the men said), Chris and I on our own for Woody Allen and an intimate tête-à-tête over kebabs, Brian and Chris for drinks any night nobody else was going out (plotting my overthrow, Berry said) and all of us, plus children, for the panto.

Berry was growing ever more radical. The next summer, she told me, she wasn't even going to shave her legs (armpits had been au naturelle for some time), though she would consider bleaching the hairs if sunlight didn't do it for her. I hardly liked to remind her (though I did) that I hadn't shaved mine for years, because I thought stubble so much less attractive than hairiness; but then my body hair is a lot fairer than hers so I was crowing from a privileged position.

More seriously, she had become an active member of CND and the women's peace movement, and had had to solemnly promise the children she wouldn't get arrested in any of their more subversive enterprises, otherwise they worried, especially after seeing demonstrations and other reminders on the television. Jamie was splendidly and unashamedly inconsistent about military matters. One minute he was telling you importantly how wicked wars were, and pasting CND stickers all over his bike, and the next he was bouncing round the house making startlingly realistic exploding noises, and brutally machine-gunning Zoe's dolls and teddies. The most public demonstration of this versatility occurred the time Berry took both children on a carnival procession through town, carrying cardboard peace doves on long poles. When they reached the park where the procession ended Jamie and another small boy started ferociously duelling with their peace doves, a sedition observed with great amusement by the carnival crowd, and causing Berry and the other boy's father severe embarrassment.

Brian didn't join in these activities. He was basically sympathetic, but he has a horror of making an exhibition of himself in public, and couldn't accompany Berry to evening meetings because someone had to babysit. He was a member (in name at least) of Friends of the Earth, and of course he's a stalwart of the Labour Party, so any energy left after a day's work he put into those. He's always been happier with the more conventional and hierarchical organizations anyway. He likes knowing where he stands, and who's responsible for what, and prefers to work within the system.

With all this talk of action and campaigns Berry made me ashamed I wasn't doing more in London; she worked too, after all, even if it was part-time, and she had the children and yet still seemed to find time for these other interests. I was sure it had something to do with the period she had off work before the children went to school. There seemed to be a squad of women who'd got to know each other very closely at a time when their experiences were shared, got radicalized together, and then drifted as a group into various organizations, and though most of them were now back at work the solidarity and commitment lingered on. I'd never had the experience of mixing with women on the domestic front; no long talks at mothers and toddlers or playgroup about the politics of breast-feeding, or the meat-inspection atmosphere at hospital clinics, and my evenings, those I wasn't working, were reserved for play and relaxation. I told myself that if I joined anything I would want to be properly involved, not just a face at meetings, and that I daren't make that kind of whole-hearted commitment; which was spectacularly wet of me, as Berry contemptuously observed, but there you are.

Chris returned to London before me to have his daughters for the last few days of their holiday, and I hung on till Jamie and Zoe went back to school and then came home myself, a week before our own term started.

After I had unpacked I pottered down to the middle flat where I could hear Harry working with the radio on. I thanked him for looking after my house plants and enquired how work on the bike was progressing. Pretty well, he said, with the end now in sight, though the accompanying sigh made him sound almost regretful about it.

I took him down a cup of coffee, and became mesmerized by watching him work, as I had been all those months ago when he'd mended my front door. He was so neat and well organized. He'd spread a huge sheet of plastic on the floor – Visqueen, he called it, sold for damp-proof courses – covered it with newspaper, and then laid everything out meticulously on top. He worked kneeling, tools close to hand, with blocks of wood in front of him as makeshift workbenches, one with a vice attached to hold parts steady. I know nothing about engines and couldn't have told a carburettor from a fuel pump (though perhaps bikes don't need the latter, with the petrol sitting on top like that) but then it wasn't the bike I was fascinated by, but Harry. It sounds silly, and ridiculously romantic – it must have been a scene reproduced in busy backwaters up and down the country – but I found myself actually moved. Such patience and single-minded devotion. I found it impossible not to smile as I watched, and it wasn't because anything was funny.

★

I went down quite often after that, while the final stages were being completed, with a cup of coffee as an excuse. I didn't stay long, partly because I didn't want to be a nuisance (though he never gave me the impression I was) but also because it was bitterly cold down there. Harry treated it as outdoors and wore thick clothes – and anyway was so absorbed in what he was doing he probably wouldn't have noticed himself icing solid – but I never remembered to put my coat on before I went down. I would stay just long enough for a progress report and a few moments of companionable silence, and then retreat to the warmth of the electric fire upstairs.

I wasn't there for the great moment. Indeed I suspect Harry might have planned it as a private climax; not because he anticipated failure but because it was such a personal matter between him and the bike. I was aware of parts reappearing on the now gleaming frame outside, but I never heard test running or anything like that. Then one February afternoon after work, carrying a rubbish bag down the fire escape, I looked below and saw the bike had gone.

I told myself, after a horrorstruck split-second, that for it to be stolen at this crucial moment would have to be excessively unlucky. I went back up to the flat but kept an eye out, and about an hour later it returned, preceded by its noise, an unusual deep thudding sound, and ridden by a sinister-looking creature in gauntlets, leather jacket and full-face black helmet, who could have been anybody, but turned out to be Harry.

He cut the engine and dismounted, hoiked the machine up on to its stand, and then took off his helmet and stood there, gazing at it.

I was by now standing on the fire escape platform outside

my back door. I leant over and called, 'So it goes then, does it?'

He looked up at me with a peculiar expression on his face, half triumphant, half reluctant, stared again at the bike, and then said briefly, 'Yes, it does.'

Of course when he said that he didn't mean it was finished. There were, naturally, dozens of fine adjustments to be made, and oil changes and other messy procedures to be undertaken, as indeed there seemed to be all the time he had the bike. Whether he simply couldn't keep his hands off it or whether it really did need so much attention I have no way of knowing, though I'd guess that bikes do genuinely demand more owner-participation than cars. Possibly they are designed like that, to add to the fun. I could certainly see that it was important that a bike as large and heavy as the AJS started easily. It had no electric ignition, and turning it over was quite an athletic exercise. I doubt I could have done it at all, and even Harry seemed to have to use his whole weight, and considerable energy, to kick it into life.

He took me for a ride on it on the Saturday. Just a short spin by his standards – he didn't use it for piffling rides about town: said it was bad for the engine and you might as well have a Honda 50 if that was all you wanted a bike for – we went out to St Albans and back.

He suggested it, and I almost said no, because although I knew I wanted to I was ashamed of such an adolescent desire. Also I was afraid I might do the wrong thing, or fall off the back; not a completely unrealistic fear, I discovered; unlikely under way, but just possible when first moving off, if you weren't ready for it, and holding on to something. I hadn't been on a bike for years (and never on anything so big) but I was aware that passengers were expected to assist (or at least not hamper) the driving process, by leaning in to corners and generally behaving themselves.

I warned Harry I wasn't experienced but he said not to worry, he wasn't going to hurl it around with me on the back, and that if I held on to him rather than the rail behind me I should be able to feel the right movements naturally.

I wore Ruth's crash helmet, which was identical to Harry's and, from the moment I climbed aboard, found the experience a revelation. Or rather, a series of revelations.

To begin with, it became immediately apparent that to be pressed up against and clinging to the person in front of you, as I was, is a curiously intimate thing to do with a man one is not otherwise on touching terms with, and was only un-embarrassing because the arrangement ensured it was a private intimacy, in that we couldn't see each other's faces, or do much talking.

Then, as we bumped down the pavement and accelerated away, I was hit by a much more powerful realization: that of my complete dependence for survival on the skills of the driver. I am aware of this as a passenger in a car – and certainly was with Chris, when I kept my eyes riveted to the road ahead, and stamped the floor involuntarily when I knew we should be braking – but I felt it much more acutely on the bike. Felt it literally; to be actually holding on to the driver's body as he negotiated a path through the hurtling world and its dangers made it impossible to forget.

But despite this, after the first minutes of strangeness and the first few corners – which I did find alarming, though more in anticipation than execution – I started to enjoy myself. As a driver Harry inspired confidence. He wasn't cautious; he used the accelerator as much as the brake in mildly hazardous manoeuvres (the traffic crossing the North

Circular is never other than mildly hazardous) but as his passenger I felt he knew exactly what he was doing, and had created more than enough time to do it in, so that none of our actions felt dictated by the unforeseen actions of others. He didn't hug the bumpers of cars while waiting to overtake them, and although we didn't stay within the speed limit – we'd have been mown down by the other traffic if we had – he resisted the temptation to open out to positively immoral speeds.

It wasn't until we were cruising the busy shopping streets of St Albans that I appreciated something else: that we were gloriously anonymous. People notice bikes, especially big old-fashioned ones, but not their riders, because they can't. Possibly I could have been identified as female, but no more than that. So while we could see everybody else and place them accordingly, they couldn't do the same to us, except in blanket terms, as bikers. Inside the helmet I could have been anyone, and this idea I found not only amusing, but peculiarly liberating. To wear a helmet is in effect to wear a mask, and the disguise, like all disguises, frees one from the normal limits of one's behaviour. Not, of course, that I behaved in any way outrageously on the journey, but I did feel that in some sense I had been released from myself, and could have been capable of actions I would never otherwise have entertained.

A funny and rather revealing incident occurred when we were almost home again. At least Harry thought it was funny, and at the time I did, too, though afterwards I wasn't so sure. Especially as Harry was the initiator, and, being an experienced biker, must have had some inkling as to what the result would be.

We drew up at the traffic lights down the road from the flats, and who should be next to us (on our left, because we were in the middle of the road) but Mr Rosen in his Escort. He was so low in the driver's seat I was surprised he could see anything over the dash at all. But he could certainly see out of the side window, just as we could see in. Harry noticed who it was – he lowered his head to squint into the car – and then reached out, tapped the window with his gloved knuckles and gave Mr Rosen a little wave.

It wasn't in any sense a threatening gesture, viewed from outside, merely a small neighbourly greeting, but it was evidently open to different interpretation from within. As Mr Rosen glanced round, an expression of terror came over his face. His hand reached for the window winder, which he jerked at feverishly to ensure it was up, and then he gripped the steering wheel with desperation and refused to look in our direction at all.

Wow, I thought, if perfectly ordinary motorcycling gear can produce that reaction, why bother with death heads and swastikas? It was a forceful example of how intuitively frightened some people are of bikers. The price of that anonymity, maybe, to be tainted by the dangerous image of the few. It was a novel experience for me, to be if not myself the object of fear at least seen to be in league with it. I would have been horrified if I hadn't found it so preposterous.

There was nothing we could do to improve the situation without frightening Mr Rosen further. We had to sit there till the lights changed, willing him not to have a seizure, and then Harry pulled off smartly in front of him, raised his hand in backward salute, and swept into the access path to the flats.

Mr Rosen must have felt foolish then, because he would have realized who it was; but he would have been relieved, too, and I was glad for him. I wouldn't have wanted him believing some mysterious biker out for his blood was loose on the roads. All the way from the lights I could feel Harry's back shaking, and I was laughing too, but perhaps it wasn't very nice of us.

# Chapter 7

You'd have thought that once Harry had successfully completed his magnum opus he would have been on permanent cloud nine, but in fact it didn't turn out that way. I suppose there's always a danger of let-down when a project important to us is finished, and although he could now go roaring off around the country – he thought nothing of going to Wales for the day, via the A40 because he found motorways boring – nevertheless he couldn't spend every waking hour on the road, and doubtless there was a sudden emptiness in his life that he hadn't yet worked out how to fill. That was what I put it down to, anyway. The climax to this reactive type of depression came about before I'd appreciated he'd gone into it, and since it was also the end of it, it wasn't until afterwards that I could look back and ascribe cause and effect. Indeed if I hadn't decided to go home that afternoon and skip a wordprocessing course at college which by rights I should have been attending, I would have missed it altogether.

The moment I stepped through the lobby doors of the flats I smelt burning. Not the dangerous bonfire or boiler type, more the culinary variety. I thought, well, I'm glad I don't have to eat that, and was just mounting the first flight of stairs when it occurred to me that it was an unHarry-like thing to do, to burn food. He wasn't an ambitious cook, but what he could do he did well, and efficiently. Moreover, it was two-thirty in the afternoon; not really a time one would expect anyone to be destroying food. And on top of that I suddenly realized that the place was unusually quiet, which might mean that there was no one in the flat to deal with whatever had happened.

Never mind being labelled a busy-body, I thought; after all, if they go up in flames I shall too, so I retraced my steps and rapped on the door. There was no reply. This concerned me a little, so I cautiously pushed open the letter-box flap, hoping a peek inside would reassure me. Probably it had happened hours ago, and the smell was just lingering on; kitchen disasters are a bit like that. But what I saw as I crouched down was anything but reassuring. The whole flat – or as much as I could see of it – was filled with smoke. Not thick smoke, admittedly, but smoke none the less, and in the doorway of the kitchen I could see feet. Not standing feet, but lying-down feet.

I dropped the flap and flew to the lobby doors, intending to race round the back; and as I met the outside air I spotted the gangling figure of the Williams boy emerging from the main entrance.

'Paul!' I shrieked. 'Help me! There's someone collapsed in the flat!'

He looked startled and glanced over his shoulder, as if expecting to see someone else called Paul standing just behind him. He should have been a mathematician, this boy, with his inner-worldly air and dreadful horn-rimmed glasses; instead, unbelievably, he was an art student.

'Paul!' I yelled again, and this time he recognized himself, and lolloped across the grass towards me.

We tore round the back and found the door not only unlocked but ajar. This explained why there wasn't more smoke in the flat, since most of it was billowing out towards us.

'Christ, what is it?' asked Paul, pulling a disgusted face.

'Food, I think.' I stood well back to push the door open. Through the smoke I could just make out a gas flame on the cooker. 'Ready?' I asked. Paul nodded.

We charged in. Paul opened the window, and I turned off the cooker and dumped the red-hot remains of what had probably been a saucepan of curry into the sink (with spectacular results – it should have gone outside but was too hot to carry that far). Lurking under the more obvious charring stench I detected another smell, more suspiciously familiar than burnt curry. Once the saucepan was dealt with, we turned our attention to the disabled culprit.

He was sitting on the floor with his back propped against the wide-open kitchen door, a spirit bottle beside him, empty and toppled. His head hung forward, chin almost touching his chest. I thought he was unconscious, till his hand lifted to brush his cheek.

I squatted in front of him and fanned aside the blast of whisky fumes. 'You're lucky the door was open,' I said grimly. 'Bloody lucky.'

'He's drunk!' Paul said, picking up the bottle and sounding shocked.

'Shit,' Harry sighed. His eyes were closed, smoke tears streaming from beneath his lashes. He coughed feebly.

'Blotto,' said Paul with distaste. He placed the bottle on the table, exuding disapproval. To look at him you'd have thought he'd never seen anyone in the advanced stages of inebriation. Or maybe, and I recall the attitude myself, he was hypocritically less tolerant of behaviour in people he regarded as fully fledged adults than he was of the same behaviour in his own peer group. Either way, while fairly intolerant of drunkenness myself, committed at any age, his attitude made me less reproving towards Harry than I might otherwise have been.

'Can you get up, Harry?' I asked. I shook his shoulder. 'Harry? It's Jane. Can you get up?'

Harry lifted his head. He was clearly in no condition to notice what our attitudes were, or care, if he had noticed. He opened his eyes, smiled at me, and then slid sideways almost gracefully into a heap in the doorway.

Paul looked as if he would have been happy to leave him to sleep it off on the floor, but I imagined Ruth returning and thought what a fright it would give her, if only for a few seconds.

'Help me get him to the bedroom,' I said decisively. 'We can't leave him here.'

Paul didn't say 'why not?', because he wasn't brave enough. He lip-curled instead, as he bent down to help.

Harry claimed afterwards that he weighed only twelve stones but, trying to lift him, I could have believed twenty. Paul, regrettably, did not surprise me with unguessed masculine strength, though squeamishness may have inhibited him. We had no success with bodily lifting, but more in hauling upright, and after that it became easier, because a vertical perspective seemed to revive Harry a little. With his arms across our shoulders we stumbled him into the hall, negotiated a ninety-degree turn into the bedroom, and lurched the last few steps to the bed. We laid him untidily on top of the quilt.

From then on it would have been simpler if he had been nearer unconsciousness. I don't like leaving drunks on their backs in case they're sick, but each time I pushed him on to his side he immediately rolled back again, as if we were playing some idiotically repetitive children's game. Behind me Paul began to make impatient noises.

'You go,' I said irritably, waving him away. 'I'll hang on till he's settled down.'

'Right,' he said, making for the door.

'Thanks,' I called after him. I heard the front door open, then slam.

I gave up the roll-over game and returned to the kitchen to fetch the washing-up bowl. A small crash and a series of thuds sent me hurrying back. I found Harry struggling to sit up, and the bedside lamp and a pile of books on the floor.

'Lie back, Harry,' I said firmly. 'You're drunk.'

'I know, I know,' he said, in an aggrieved tone, as if someone other than himself had been responsible for it; but he did lie back. I picked up the lamp, unplugged it from the wall and removed it to a chest of drawers.

'Where's Ruth?' he asked suddenly.

'At work,' I said, stacking the books next to the lamp. 'Go to sleep.'

'When will she be back?' His speech was perfectly distinct, but laboured, as if it was selection of words he found difficult, not their articulation.

'Not for hours,' I said patiently. 'Please go to sleep.'

He stared up at the ceiling a moment.

'One day,' he said, 'Ruth's going to give me a baby.'

I swung round to look at him. 'Is she?' I said, and started to feel a little sorry for him, because I doubted she was. I walked over to the bed and sat down beside him. 'That's nice,' I said kindly, and patted his arm.

He smiled at the ceiling, then dropped his gaze to me. A look of vague hopefulness dawned.

'Are you going to give me a baby?' He brightened, as if it were something I might be going to effect immediately.

'I think that's most unlikely,' I said. He looked disappointed. 'Though you never can tell,' I added encouragingly, knowing it's always good policy to humour drunks.

'No.' He gave a serious nod, then switched his attention to

the open bedroom door. He frowned, and sniffed the air. 'Actually,' he said, with a guarded glance back at me. 'I'm not really hungry.'

'What?' I felt the beginnings of a laugh.

He sniffed the air again. 'Shit,' he complained. 'You've burnt it, haven't you?'

From then on I began to enjoy myself. Harry was a most unbelligerent and charmingly inconsequential drunk. It was rather fun trying to follow the mental leaps, especially knowing I could say anything that entered my head in reply, since it was immediately consigned to oblivion.

He did become a little maudlin at one point, about children again, but it didn't last long, and then he must have been reminded how children are made, because he became quite affectionate; and since I felt quite affectionate towards him at the time, I let him kiss me. Not without a twinge of guilt, but I knew he wasn't capable of anything more treacherous, and, as I say, I'm a firm believer in humouring drunks . . . actually that's a lie; I wouldn't let Chris make love to me when he was drunk – which he rarely was, I hasten to add – and generally speaking I find something vaguely disgusting about drunken men on the job: all that dead weight and grunting and conviction they can do it when you know perfectly well it's going to go on boringly for hours and they're going to fall asleep on top of you before they get anywhere.

But a kiss is all right, even if it is neat whisky, and for once I actually enjoyed the sensation of heaviness against me, because it was an unfamiliar body, I suppose, and because however much faithful couples try to convince you otherwise, you can't beat unfamiliarity for excitement where these things are concerned.

Eventually Harry drifted off, looking rather ill, pasty and damp. I carefully removed his arm from my waist and covered him with the bits of the duvet he wasn't lying on. I felt a familiar tenderness doing this. I don't know why I find sleeping men so touching – because they're so terrified of appearing off-guard and vulnerable when awake, I suspect. I once told Berry I wouldn't mind living with a sleeping man; except of course they refuse to stay that way.

Back in the kitchen I disposed of the ruined saucepan and whisky bottle. I thought of ringing Ruth to warn her what she was coming home to but although I found an address book by the phone there didn't seem to be any prominent entries at the front, where people usually put work numbers, and I couldn't face going through the whole book. I settled for dolloping Ajax cream on the cooker, took a last check on Harry to make sure he was still on his side, and then feeling I had done all that could be reasonably expected of a neighbour and friend (and guiltily amused, even a fraction more) let myself out the front door.

Upstairs, preparing my own supper, I remembered the burnt curry and guessed it had been theirs, which would mean Ruth coming home hungry to nothing. So I made a double quantity of spaghetti sauce which I could always use the next day if she had other plans.

I left my front door open and when I heard the lobby doors bang raced down and caught her just as she was letting herself in.

I explained what had happened, very casually, so as not to frighten her, but she still looked upset, though not especially surprised, as if it were something she knew he was working up to. She went in to see him, but only briefly – he was still asleep – and accepted my offer of supper gratefully, with the suggestion we ate it there, in case he awoke.

So we cooked her spaghetti and ate it with my sauce, and afterwards talked and watched the news: Lebanese killing each other, and women and children starving to death in the Horn of Africa while their menfolk waged an inexplicable war for control of that God-forsaken region.

Finally Harry awoke and wandered through, very frail and tottery, but more or less sober again; and I recognized the looks they gave each other, and left them to it.

# Chapter 8

The episode seemed to jolt Harry into remedial action and the next ten days he spent mixing concrete and humping bricks for a local builder, for which he was paid almost as much as he had earned in a month at the assessment centre before Christmas. Then he and Ruth went on holiday to Crete, leaving the bike under lock and key at a nearby garage. I was astounded when he told me how much it was now worth; not in the Vincent league, he told me, but it had still become a real collectors' item.

Their holiday coincided with the schools' half-term, and Jamie and Zoe were bitterly disappointed that neither Harry nor the bike were around for their entertainment. They liked Chris and were used to him – and if the need arose I was happy to leave him in charge, because he'd mastered the feminine art of doing several things at the same time, so he didn't get flustered or forget about them while he was doing something else. But they regarded him rather as they did me, as a secure and dependable adult as likely to be issuing orders as providing treats, and took him similarly for granted, rather than as a large human plaything as they did Harry. That's always the way with children; it's much easier to be popular with them when you're not the one with the responsibility.

After half-term a certain tension crept into my relationship with Chris, and I found myself starting to consider life without him. I didn't want to end it there and then, but I caught myself speculating on the possibility, which is always a bad sign. This tension was precipitated by his involvement in a serious car accident, and fostered by his complete inability to admit, even to me, that he might have been in any way to blame.

It happened during the fortnight Ruth and Harry were away, when Chris was returning home after an evening class. I wasn't with him, so I didn't know the precise details, but the sequence of events appeared to have been that he was approaching traffic lights at some speed, gambled on them changing before he got there, which they did, but only just, and a car containing a man and his girlfriend that was in the middle of the junction waiting to turn right was hit by him with considerable force on its passenger side. There was a lot of other traffic about, and it was wet and dark, but, still, the car was stationary and the girl in the front seat was badly injured, and both the cars were write-offs. To complicate matters the man had been drinking and failed the breath test (which Chris didn't) and Chris used this fact too to shift blame from himself, despite no one's suggestion that the man had committed any traffic offence because of it.

Chris was furious and upset when the police said they were going to bring charges against him. When I told him I thought driving without due care and attention a singularly mild charge to face, considering the consequences, he was furious with me too, for not being more supportive and loyal. Of course he was very shaken up by the accident and desperately sorry for the girl, even going to see her in hospital, which a lot of other drivers wouldn't have done. But while I could understand him not admitting guilt in public (indeed his insurance company insisted on it) I was shocked that he wouldn't face up to it in private. I began to sense the onset of that panicky cold-feet feeling that comes when you are forced to acknowledge fundamental weaknesses in a partner, and know them to be important.

The tension climaxed into a bitterly hissed row in the canteen one lunchtime when I told him what a lousy driver he was and how I hated being driven by him, and he argued back, scarlet in the face with outrage (anyone would have thought it was his sexual rather than driving performance I was criticizing), that he hadn't broken any speed limit or jumped the lights, and it had been his right of way; in short completely overlooking the indisputable facts (a) that he had failed to notice a large and vulnerable object in his path, and (b) that however much he was within the law he still shouldn't have careered straight into it.

If he had just said: I don't know why I didn't see it; and accepted that in London you can't drive around blithely assuming traffic is always going to be where it should be under text-book conditions, I would have been more sympathetic. We all make mistakes, and we can't all be brilliant drivers. But we can at least acknowledge our limitations, and it was his failure to do this that made me so angry; it seemed so utterly wilful and obstructive.

The colluding attitude of the insurance company appalled me too, allowing him the very day after the accident, before we knew what he was going to be charged with and while the girl was still in a critical condition in hospital, to hire a replacement car on his policy. Perhaps it was irrational of me, but I couldn't help thinking that if the car had been a machine gun, and he'd pointed it at someone and shot them, he'd hardly have been handed another the next day, before it had been established whether the action had been negligent or not.

The affair caused weeks of ill-feeling undoubtedly made worse by the fact that, given a car, I am a reasonably proficient driver. I'm quite fast and assertive – you'd never make a right turn at all in London if you weren't – but I have good anticipation, fast reactions, and can park competently in a space only a few feet longer than the car. I kept telling Chris that there was no mystery about the latter, and if he just followed the rules and didn't rush it he couldn't go wrong, but he didn't want to be told and would have much preferred it if I had been a non-driver, and not in a position to criticize.

Anyway, the upshot of it all was that the girl pulled through and seemed set to make a full recovery, though she had had a wretched time of it, with two broken legs and assorted other less major injuries; the man driving her stood to be fined and banned for a year because of the drink; and Chris was advised to expect a fine and to collect a number of points under the totting-up system. It seemed to me that suffering was being distributed in exact inverse proportion to the culpability of the parties involved, and made me very cross.

But I did continue to see Chris and although I berated him about it in private I kept my feelings to myself in company. When Ruth and Harry returned from Crete I told them what had happened but no more, which meant that during an evening we spent together Chris got some polite sympathy from them. And it turned out that Harry had had a number of bike spills in the past and even ended up in hospital with concussion on one occasion, so they could swap accident stories which for once gave them something in common to talk about. Moreover, Harry's fatalistic biker's view, that it was impossible to keep out of the way of all the morons on the road, and that the most you could do was strive to minimize the risks as best you could, seemed to give Chris some comfort, though I couldn't imagine why; presumably he didn't associate himself with the morons.

He came back up to the flat afterwards, saying that perhaps that bloke wasn't so bad, when you got to know him, though he still couldn't see what a classy girl like Ruth saw in him (Ruth wasn't a girl but no matter, it just meant Chris fancied her) when she could obviously have done so much better for herself.

I thought this remark downright bitchy, and, considering how much Harry's non-judgemental attitude and general solidarity had contributed to Chris's improved spirits over the evening, showed exceptional meanness of character. So I said, 'Maybe he's terrific in the sack,' which irritated Chris intensely, because he disliked women making crude sexual references (unless they were about him, and said in bed), and also because he so clearly found Ruth attractive himself and probably didn't like to imagine her wasting her libido on someone as uninteresting and blatantly masculine as Harry.

Chris's attitude to Harry at that time was curious altogether: in his presence he made a conspicuous effort with him and always seemed pleased when they agreed on things, as if he wanted to be identified with him in some way, and yet when we were alone he made snide and denigrating comments about him, often quite gratuitously and with surprising vehemence. He wasn't usually like this unless uncomfortable emotions were involved – as, say, in his relationship with his ex-wife – and though I accepted that Harry had a knack of inspiring negative responses I suspected that in Chris's case this was heightened by a legacy from the fight incident. I guessed that the muddle of feelings aroused in him then, his anger and sense of loss of prestige, mixed in with a grudging admiration for Harry, served to make their relationship very ambivalent. (Ambivalent on Chris's side, that is; I doubt Harry gave a moment's thought, even subconsciously, to anything as abstract as the nature or quality of his relationships with others.)

But a lot of things Harry did Chris seemed to find confusing, too. They appeared to him mysterious and whimsical and he would scorn them, but at the same time leave you with the feeling that there must be something admirable in them to elicit such a reaction, and that Chris could see this too and was scornful merely because he couldn't bring himself to be impressed.

Like the time one of the young offenders turned up at Ruth and Harry's flat, just before Easter. The boy banged on their door late in the evening, announced he'd absconded and demanded Harry's help. Harry said, 'Not likely,' but agreed not to turn him in till the morning, and then, because it seemed a waste for the boy to spend his one night of liberty asleep, drove him down to the Gower peninsula on the bike – a three-hour trip each way – and they roared around the dunes in the dead of a chilly night and returned at seven trailing sand all over the place. (Which meant that after Harry had taken the boy back and told him he'd get a different reception if he tried it again, he had to spend hours removing every last trace of sand from the bike, a task he probably enjoyed quite as much as the ride.)

Chris looked nonplussed when I told him this story (which I thought displayed an unsuspectedly sensitive and even romantic side to Harry's nature) and then fought some internal battle with his emotions, impressive evidence of which could be seen in the contortions of his expression while the conflict raged, and which ended, rejection triumphant, with him muttering, 'Well, he doesn't have to get up for work in the morning, does he?'

As a statement of fact it was true, at that particular time, but it was also, I thought, probably irrelevant.

★

At Easter Chris took his daughters down to Cornwall to stay in a cottage for a week. He wanted me to go with him, and I had been in the past, but I didn't really enjoy playing mother to them (a role he always seemed to encourage me to practise) and this year especially I didn't want to.

Instead I decided on a whistle-stop tour of friends and relatives, starting on Good Friday with Norwich; and when I told Harry I was offered a lift up there. He hadn't had a spin on the Norfolk roads for years, he claimed, and it would only take a couple of hours and a few quid on petrol.

I hesitated, because the idea seemed so outlandish, and then, attracted for precisely that reason, impulsively agreed, as long as the weather was fine.

When I rang Berry to tell her that she probably wouldn't have to meet me at the station, and why, she said I must be mad, but that the children would be delighted, and of course Harry must stay for lunch and meet her and Brian. I accepted for him because I couldn't believe he would want simply to drop me off and head straight home and, when I told him, was irritated that he didn't sound more enthusiastic.

'You don't have to, you know,' I said sourly. 'You're not doing them a bloody favour.'

He looked taken aback, as if people didn't normally criticize him for his churlishness, before replying defensively, 'No, OK. Be nice to see the kids anyway.'

The night before we left I switched on the television at half nine for the weather forecast; Easter was late that year and the week had been glorious, but I wanted to be absolutely sure it would hold.

Before the weather man appeared I caught the last item of news and was stunned by an image from the streets of Beirut. A bareheaded and beautiful young man was standing braced and urgent, in the centre of a city street: a ruined street, but a still-living street, and a once-civilized street, with fine buildings and apartment blocks; and he was spraying the opposite side of the road with machine gun fire. Behind him civilians – women and children – scurried on their way, some carrying bags that looked like shopping bags, and at his feet lay a dead comrade. They didn't show us who he was firing at, or explain why that side of the street was the enemy, or who the enemy might have been, and the street could have been from a city anywhere in the world. The children were still going to school; they said a school bus had been hit by mortar fire. I found it unbelievable.

The following morning Harry compromised his principles by using the A1M as far as Baldock, because it's the only sensible route out from Kilburn, and then we skirted south of Cambridge and north of Newmarket and ripped through Thetford Forest on the A11. The roads are a trifle straight for a devotee cyclist like Harry, but the later sections are all single carriageway and were teeming with Bank Holiday traffic, so there was plenty of overtaking and other diversions to keep him happy. The weather was perfect, cloudless skies and not too many insects that early in the year, and the bike behaved itself beautifully; I felt exhilarated and free, and a quite different person. Entering Norwich I was afflicted with post-heroic silliness and found myself wishing Harry would roar around more; however, he was boringly responsible and trundled the bike into the residential streets at a frustratingly inoffensive pace.

Brian and Berry lived at that time in a large Victorian semi off the inner ring road, bought for peanuts in the days when East Anglians had straw in their hair and the university down the road had only just emerged from its sea of mud. Our approach to the house may have been disappointingly sedate, but our arrival was everything I could have childishly hoped for.

Brian and Jamie were both in the low-hedged front garden, Jamie with his push bike and Brian with the lawn mower, and the expressions on their faces as we thudded towards them were a delight. I think at that moment Harry was elevated to the status of god in Jamie's eyes. He stood transfixed, with his mouth wide open, as if he didn't dare believe that this heavenly vehicle was going to stop at his home; and the expression on Brian's face was just as fascinating, though more complicated. Shades of Chris: part of it mirrored his son's reaction, but another more responsibly adult part fought it, and the result was delicious: a masterpiece of contradiction.

I suspected that even I, because of my association with the keeper of this glorious machine, acquired the temporary lustre of a lesser deity; when I dismounted and took off Ruth's helmet to shake out my hair Jamie stared at me as if he had never properly seen me before.

Harry drove further up the gravel drive, cut the engine and lifted the bike on to its stand, watched intently by Jamie, and, with more guarded interest, by Brian. He removed his helmet and turned to survey his audience.

'Hello, Jamie,' he said gravely.

'Hello,' Jamie breathed. He hesitated, and then, suddenly galvanized with enthusiasm, turned to his father. 'This is Harry,' he announced.

'Hello,' said Brian cautiously, and with an indecipherable note of reappraisal. Despite the half-shorn appearance of the tiny front lawn he disconnected the mower flex and started to bundle it over his arm. It unfairly crossed my mind that, politeness notwithstanding, nothing would have now persuaded him to be seen driving a lawn mower.

'Careful,' said Harry to Jamie, catching him before he touched the motorbike. 'It's hot.'

Jamie nodded and folded his arms to inspect it instead, man to man.

'Well, hi!' said Berry's voice. We all turned to see her standing at the front door, in jeans and a pink sweatshirt, beside a beaming Zoe. She stepped down on to the gravel, looked at me and Harry, and then sparklingly at her two males, and burst out laughing.

It wasn't Harry's fault that he wasn't the person Brian expected him to be, nor that this fact, combined with Brian's liking for Chris and mistrust of me, should have conspired to raise immediate suspicions in my brother-in-law's mind. I had anticipated none of these complications and was initially baffled by his wariness and uncharacteristic stiffness towards us. Only later did I discover that on quite insufficient evidence – perhaps from something the children had said that he had misconstrued, or possibly some remark I myself had made at Christmas – he had jumped to the conclusion that Harry was a social worker, a breed the males of which he contemptuously views as intrinsically sexless and safe; he was therefore both disconcerted and affronted to be presented with an imposter who was clearly neither sexless nor conspicuously safe, and nor, as he soon realized to his indignant dismay, even a social worker.

I then compounded his ill-humour, as we sipped pre-lunch Martinis on the terrace overlooking their huge back garden, by making passing and disapproving reference to Chris's car crash. Brian immediately and aggressively sprang to Chris's defence, which at the time I put down to irrational solidarity among male car drivers; however, later, and with other facts to hand, I realized that the vehemence was provoked by my treachery in criticizing my partner – and his friend – in front of a man whose crude appeal I could not be trusted to resist, and with whom I had already committed the near-adulterous offence of riding pillion. And of course Brian's partisanship merely extended the argument and incensed me into complaints far more vituperative than I would normally have considered fair, in front of others.

But as a result the few remarks he addressed directly to Harry over lunch, which we also had in the garden, the children banished with mountainous plates to their den behind an apple tree, were of an unfriendly and hectoring nature, not far short of belligerent. Mostly, too, of the pompously long-winded type that demanded only yes or no answers, which given Harry's difficulties with small talk at the best of times, were consequently all he got.

'The children tell me,' he said at one point, helping himself to a second bowlful of chocolate mousse despite Berry's frown, 'that you've spent months getting that bike on the road.' He glanced across at Harry innocently. 'Most of the winter, I understand?'

'Yeah,' said Harry, nodding at the plate on his lap. This was at least a variation in reply, as it had just been revealed by a series of monosyllabic negatives that he definitely wasn't, had never been, and wasn't planning to be, a social worker.

'It's worth it now, is it?' Brian persisted. 'I mean, after all that work? You find it more useful than, say . . .' he hesitated '. . . a car?' The timing of this suggested an incipient *coup de grâce*, though the winning angle was unclear. Brian himself owned a VW Passat, of whose sporting performance and mechanical sophistication he was tediously proud.

Harry shrugged and looked away. I thought it a gesture of helplessness in the face of what must have seemed an inexplicable hostility, but it's possible that to someone who knew him less well it could have suggested indifference, or worse still, contempt.

Brian, watching him closely, bristled. 'Or perhaps usefulness doesn't come into it,' he pressed on grimly. 'I suppose it's a matter, ultimately, of what you want a vehicle for.'

I suddenly grasped the angle – Poseur versus Practical Man – and bristled myself.

Harry shrugged again, this time diffidently.

'Only got a licence for a bike,' he said.

'Oh,' said Brian. For a moment he looked cheated. Then he said, 'Ah,' and nodded, deciding to accept victory anyway, even from an unexpected quarter, and leant back in triumph.

Berry and I immediately launched into conversation on a different topic; not for the first time during the meal, or the last.

After lunch Harry escaped to play violent games with the children at the bottom of the lawn, while Berry and I chatted in deck chairs by the house. Brian lolled on the grass beside us, uninterested in our conversation, watching his children wrestle their willing victim to the ground and subject him to the unmalicious and exuberant savagery only small children are capable of. After a while he went over and tried to join in the fun, but the children definitely preferred the idea of beating up Harry; his forays were spurned with cries of, 'Let me go, Daddy, I'm fighting Harry!' and soon he wandered back defeated.

Berry and I watched this performance and I caught my sister's lips twitching, partly in sympathy with Brian for his children's tactlessness and partly out of spiteful amusement. Brian rarely played this sort of game with his children, and I guessed that if she thought some kind of competition was going on he had got no better than he deserved.

★

Berry and I know each other extraordinarily well. We aren't very alike, either in looks or character, but I can often anticipate what she's going to say before she says it, and I daresay she could finish most of my sentences for me, if she were that impolite. She's shorter than I am and darker, wears her hair cropped, is very slim, and, unlike me, is almost bustless. This last hasn't always been the case, but occurred after motherhood, much to Brian's disappointment, as he has always been a bosom man. Within the space of twelve months, from Zoe's birth to a few weeks after she stopped breastfeeding, she shrank from 38DD to 34 pre-literal, and there was nothing anyone could do about it. Such are the mysteries of women's bodies.

In character she's a person given to instant judgements of others and she's usually right, or at least she's better at it than I am. But the disadvantage of this is that she ends up not looking very deeply into anyone. She'll say, 'She's a super lady' or 'He's a real creep' (it tends to be that way round) and that's how they stay, because she's made up her mind. It takes me much longer to work people out, but because of that I try harder, and I find it difficult to end up whole-heartedly disliking anybody (unless they're patently obnoxious, like Mrs Rosen) because by then I can usually see so much in them, and almost nobody is dislikeable all the way through.

As a girl Berry was popular and vivacious and flirty and cultivated a scatterbrained sexpot image, although in fact she met Brian when she was seventeen and – as far as I know – has remained faithful to him ever since; while I, who was always labelled steady and responsible, and have never mastered the art of flirting because in company I tend to forget that I too have an image to project, have ironically been the one to fail to 'settle down' and have been the one to enjoy – and I think that is the word I mean – a varied and inconstant romantic history.

The only quality we have truly in common is our sense of humour, which has always been the despair of Brian, who says we can be heard cackling like witches all over the house, and seems to make him paranoid, as if he imagines that women on their own have nothing better to talk about than men, and therefore assumes we are dissecting him or some other male specimen and roaring with laughter over the results. I originally took this reaction as peculiar to Brian, but Berry insisted it was universal among husbands. She said, for instance, that nearly all the women enrolled for the women's studies courses she helped organize reported similar problems. According to her the husbands either wrote off the courses as trivial, because it was just women talking about babies and cystitis and other boring or revolting domestica, or else viewed them as highly subversive, since the women were obviously talking about themselves and exposing the minutiae of their sexual proclivities and performance to hordes of man-hating females. She said quite a number of the women didn't tell their menfolk what the courses were about at all, for fear of scorn or objection, and allowed them to go on assuming they were knitting doilies or stuffing soft toys or whatever it was they did before they took the plunge.

Interestingly when Berry herself joined a consciousness-raising group, years before, Brian didn't appear at all threatened, though she claimed to have given him a detailed list of the issues they would be discussing. She put this down to natural arrogance on his part, and also to the fact that at the time he was worrying about the funny noises the gear box in their old Marina was making, and wasn't really listening.

## Chapter 9

Washing up after lunch with Berry in the kitchen, I expressed my anger at Brian's ungraciousness towards Harry; an unedited version of what I intended to say to my brother-in-law later. Behind me Berry added reinforcing noises, unapologetically, consistent with her view that while Brian's behaviour might at times be reprehensible it wasn't her responsibility. At present, indeed, it seemed little was: she held a tea towel as a token of domestic intent but had in fact drunk far too much alcohol to combine constructive action with conversation.

At a peak of irritation I snatched a glass from the washing-up bowl and, in passing, rapped it smartly against the overhanging mixer tap. It broke and fell into the water.

'Oh hell, I'm sorry,' I said crossly. 'It's one of your expensive ones.' I groped beneath the suds for the pieces and transferred them to the pedal bin. 'But it's so rude,' I insisted. 'God knows what Harry must think.'

'Oh, don't fuss,' sighed Berry. 'He's bearing up OK.' She seemed suddenly weary of the topic. She flicked the tea towel at a drowsy fly on the scrubbed surface of the kitchen table, missed it, and caught a vase of wallflowers in the centre. It swayed, but remained upright.

She sighed again. 'I'm sorry about Brian, but it's only because he's worried about you and Chris. First he hears you're not going to Cornwall with him and then you turn up with some strange bloke on a motorbike, and he has to listen to you slagging Chris off in front of him . . . you know what he's like . . . he hates having to get used to someone new.'

'*He* hates it!' I swung round to face her. '*He* hates it? My God, the way his mind works! Does he honestly think I'd turn up here with someone new, without a word to anyone! And I wasn't slagging Chris off, or I wouldn't have been if he hadn't turned it into such a big thing. Anyway, I wouldn't have been talking about him at all if I'd had something going with Harry, would I? Where's his commonsense, never mind his manners.'

Berry shrugged in a 'what can you expect from mere men' gesture and moved closer. 'Mind you,' she said conspiratorially, 'I wouldn't blame you. He's bloody attractive.' She giggled tipsily. 'Real mean and moody type.'

I stared at her, surprised; not by the mean and moody reference, even if that was a rather silly exaggeration, but that she rated Harry attractive. Although it's true that I've always had difficulty deciding if people I know well are good looking. When I first meet anyone I do make an assessment, and with men it's conscious, but as we get to know each other the judgements become blurred. People I thought stunningly attractive to begin with become less so (especially if I decide I don't really like them) and those I thought plain develop qualities that somehow improve them (especially if I find I like them) until everybody ends up somewhere in the middle and I have completely lost my objectivity. I can only make a renewed assessment if I see them as strangers again, perhaps catch sight of them without realizing who they are, or see them in untypical clothes or situations. But I knew I hadn't made any initial judgement of Harry as attractive; far from it. At the same time I couldn't help thinking how perverse it was of Berry, as an active feminist, to go for what she saw as the mean and brooding types. Presumably she wanted a schizophrenic arrangement where they looked one thing and acted another.

I said doubtfully, 'Do you think so?' still thinking about first impressions, and then felt dishonest. I knew I did find Harry attractive, now. Well, appealing, anyway.

'Oh yes. Great looking.' She suppressed a laugh. 'Especially when Brian was having a go at him . . .' She was on the point of saying more but caught my eye and substituted a grin. Berry enjoys this sort of conversation, but I don't and she knows it. They make me uncomfortable, probably because I don't like to imagine men discussing women in the same way. Besides, our positions are different: Berry can express as many lustful thoughts as she likes, as a married woman, without anyone expecting her to do anything about it. It feels quite different from where I stand, and unless I am really serious or actually drunk – rather than merely Martini-flushed – I prefer to keep such thoughts private. And in this case particularly, as I didn't entirely trust my sister's motives and guessed she might be hoping for indiscretions.

I re-applied myself to the dishes.

'I was surprised he couldn't drive a car,' I said after a moment, selecting what seemed a safer line of conversation.

Berry laughed incredulously. 'You believed him? God, Jane, you are naïve.'

I glanced back at her, startled. 'What d'you mean . . . why on earth should he lie?'

Berry looked scornful. 'Pre-emptive surrender. Trying to shut Brian up. Worked, too.' She ticked impatiently. 'Come on, you're not seriously telling me a man like that can't drive?'

It suddenly seemed most unlikely. I was momentarily shaken, an effect casual adult lies always have on me, and then piqued; that Berry, on the briefest acquaintance, might have read him better than I had.

I clattered on with the dishes, my mind scouring the recent conversation for springboards back to the highground.

'Anyway,' I said stubbornly, having to make do with the topic just discarded, 'his looks are deceptive. When you get to know him there's nothing particularly mean and moody about him. I think he may just be shy.'

'Oh yeah?' She sounded disbelieving. 'Well, I'd ride pillion with him any day.'

She was beside me now, staring out through the window. Down the lawn we could see Harry lying on his back, ankles crossed and arms behind his head, in an attitude of determined relaxation. Zoe, squatting by his feet, appeared to be trying to unbuckle his boots. Her face was grim with effort. Jamie zoomed in a semi-circle around them, then ran in and leapt, knees first, on to Harry's stomach. Harry jack-knifed, spilling Zoe on to the grass. Jamie bounced up and delivered two sharp kicks to Harry's side. Brian was sitting where we had left him, silent, possibly enjoying the spectacle.

Berry winced. 'Little sod. He's getting over-excited.' She opened the window wide. 'Jamie!' she called. 'If I see you do that again I'm coming to get you. Brian!' She frowned meaningfully at her husband.

Harry caught Jamie's leg and felled him with a tug, then turned his face towards us, grinning broadly.

'Hey!' Berry whispered. 'What a transformation!' She latched the window and giggled. 'Tell me again, what exactly is it he does? Now he's confessed he's not a social worker, that is.'

'Not much,' I said, drying my hands, 'except work on the bike.' I inspected the coffee level in the percolator. 'They don't have a very extravagant lifestyle, and Ruth must do OK, so he doesn't really need to bother.'

'Wow,' Berry looked impressed. 'He's the genuine article then, is he?'

She turned back to the window. Jamie had retreated to the far end of the garden and was satisfying his aggression on the fruit bushes with a large stick. Zoe was now sitting astride Harry, who was face down on the grass, passively ignoring her ministrations. Brian wandered down the lawn to rescue the fruit bushes and reclaim his son.

Berry looked at Harry's recumbent form.

'Nice warm day like this, shame we haven't persuaded him to take his T-shirt off.' She laughed self-consciously, as if she hadn't intended to say it aloud.

'Now who's getting over-excited?' I hissed. 'Do get a grip on yourself. You won't improve matters if you make Brian jealous.'

She flapped a dismissive hand at me. 'He is already, can't you tell? Look at the way he glowers at Harry when he's playing with the children. It's written all over him. Anyway . . .' She sniffed. 'What's so wrong with wanting to look at something attractive? At least he hasn't got a beer gut.' This was a pointed reference to Brian.

I frowned and rebuked her for the 'something' rather than 'someone', reminding her that she was the one always complaining about men treating women as sex objects.

But she decided to be unrepentant, except for the slip of the tongue, and told me I was confusing 'object' as in 'objective' or 'object of desire', which merely described a natural and perfectly acceptable fact of sexual life (actually she said unobjectionable, adding to the confusion) with 'object' as in 'thing', with the rightly deplored connotations of property and debasement.

I took her point, even if I wasn't entirely persuaded she hadn't veered across the tracks. Still, who doesn't like looking at something attractive; and now I've done it myself, so there you are.

We carried the coffee outside. Brian was still at the bottom of the garden, stretching and rubbing his stomach. Behind him Jamie, still wielding the stick, jabbed intermittently at raspberry canes. Berry stood the coffee pot on the table and strolled across to Harry and Zoe, lying motionless in a heap on the grass. She beckoned to me, finger to lips.

'How sweet.' She laughed quietly as I approached. 'They're asleep. Doesn't Zoe look adorable.'

Below us Harry lay insensible, his face half-buried in one arm, the other flung wide. Zoe was strewn across him, her head twisted against his shoulder, looking as if unconsciousness had overcome her mid-tackle, yet managing to appear completely relaxed and comfortable. The view of Harry was touching; of Zoe, achingly so. Gazing down at the child's pale perfection, I both envied and pitied my sister.

Berry sighed at her daughter's beauty and then, catching Brian's eye, stabbed a finger towards the coffee on the table.

On his slow way back Brian stopped by Zoe, frowned, and scooped her up. He carried her to the terrace, shushing her whimpers, and lowered her carefully on to one of the sunbeds. Berry glanced at me enigmatically but said nothing. Zoe kicked at the canvas irritably and began to moan, and either that or her removal must have woken Harry. He stirred and propped himself on his elbows to watch Berry pour out.

'Coffee?' She picked up a cup and waved it at him.

He grunted and jumped to his feet. As he walked towards us he glanced at his watch. 'Have to be off soon,' he said.

'You've time for coffee, surely?' Berry spoke with a touch of asperity, sounding a little vexed, though I wasn't sure why. Maybe it was a tactic she employed with men she found attractive.

However, it produced no reaction in Harry, but then he was probably used to it – people being mildly vexed with him, that is. He simply replied 'Sure,' dragged up a deck chair and sat down.

Berry stared at him, and then turned to me deliberately.

'I know what I meant to ask you. Have you heard anything from Joanna recently? Some of the women were asking after her.'

I shook my head. 'Not since I delivered some letters last autumn. And she wasn't very forthcoming then. I rather think I count as the tail end of a part of her life she'd prefer to forget.'

It seemed rude to discuss a topic Harry knew nothing about, so I explained.

'Joanna's a woman who stayed with me a year or so back. She used to live up here, but she had a real bully of a husband and when he went to gaol she decided to move away and disappear. London seemed the obvious place.' I smiled and pulled a face at my sister. 'Berry organized me into it.'

'Yeah?' For the first time since we had arrived Harry looked genuinely interested. 'What'd he go down for?'

'Oh, lots of things. Fraud, embezzlement, you name it. He ran a garage business and when it went bust his partner called the police in. He got two years. But it came at just the right time for Joanna. He was appallingly violent towards her.' I turned to Berry. 'You reckoned she was close to suicide, didn't you?'

Berry nodded. 'That's what we were afraid of.' She took up the story, talking to both of us, but since I knew most of it, really to Harry.

'He was one of those obsessive controllers. And paranoid. He hated all us women, really hated us. He was convinced we were driving a wedge between him and Joanna . . . he couldn't see that the more he tried to cut her off from people the more he was creating his own wedge. Classic case of someone in a real state themselves, refusing to acknowledge it, and everybody else having to pick up the pieces. Joanna thought he was untouchable by the end. Not . . .' she shook her head emphatically, '. . . the type you could serve an injunction on and get away with it. She gave up trying to take him to court. Even the third time he only got a week, and by God she paid for it when he came out . . . disgraceful, when you think they gave him two years for fraud.' She sighed. 'The trouble was, he always came across as so reasonable in court. All grovelling and "yes, your honour, no, your honour", until he'd got everybody sympathizing with him for having such a hysterical wife and wondering why she wasn't locked away in a mental hospital. And then he'd go straight home and beat her up again. By the end she could have done with a rest in an institution. At least she'd have been safe there.' She screwed up her face in disbelief. 'He honestly thought he was in the right, that's what was so frightening. I can tell you, if he'd been my husband I'd have stuck a knife in him years before and hang the consequences. She was living in a prison as it was.'

Brian snorted. 'So much for non-violence. Christ, you didn't even know the bloke. She may have made life hell for him.'

'Even if she did,' Berry replied sharply, 'and actually I think he was perfectly capable of creating his own hell, she didn't kick his teeth out or break his nose or crack his ribs.' The set of her jaw added: and you don't have to jump to his defence just because he's a man.

Brian snorted again and glanced at Harry, perhaps hoping for a glimmer of solidarity, but if so was not surprisingly disappointed. He looked away, his attitude disdainful, but not prepared to pursue it further.

We'd had these arguments before. Why Brian, who in fifteen years of marriage had never raised a finger to Berry, found it necessary to identify with ogres of his own sex, I couldn't imagine. Possibly because he felt Berry did the same with women, which to an extent was true, though in reply she would undoubtedly have argued that women need solidarity more than men, because of their weaker position, and that anyway very few women are as unambiguously ogreish as their male counterparts. Maybe also, returning to this instance, he saw domestic arguments in terms of winners and losers, and, since he probably rated women's tongues as more lethal than men's, thought that retaliation of a different kind was understandable, if not excusable.

Harry said laconically, 'Should have got some blokes together to give him a thumping. Ruth had a woman once, her husband was like that. Always promising the courts he'd be a good boy and then going straight home and laying into her again. She had three brothers and when they found out what was going on they went over and sorted him out.' His lips twitched. 'Can't say Ruth approved but it worked. They all got fined but reckoned it worth every penny. It's the only thing that'll do the trick with some people.'

Berry stared at him, uncertain how to respond to this, having just rashly recommended domestic murder herself. At last she said, 'Yes. Well. Joanna didn't have any brothers. In fact she didn't really have anyone. That was the problem.'

Harry shrugged and glanced away. Jamie came bounding up and as if determined to have the last word on the subject whacked Zoe across the thighs with his stick. She opened her mouth wide, a picture of silent agony.

Berry hissed, 'Christ, Jamie!' and put her coffee mug down. Zoe's lungs reached full expansion and released a thready wail. Brian pursed his lips, removed the stick from Jamie, and broke it across his knee. Zoe staggered across to Berry, dragging the afflicted leg behind her piteously, and buried her face in her mother's stomach. The wail subsided to sobs and gasps.

Harry perhaps sensed the onset of a general jaundiced overtiredness and stood up.

'I'd better be off, I reckon,' he said.

Jamie, who had been trying to decide whether to make an issue out of the broken stick, forgot it and leaped around him.

'Can I have a ride on the bike, Harry? Oh please . . . Mummy, can I?'

Berry regarded him with disfavour, then sighed and looked up at Harry. He frowned and said to Jamie, 'You haven't got a crash hat, have you? You can't ride without a crash hat.'

Jamie took this as meaning: if you have a crash helmet, then I will give you a ride. Instantly he said, 'I can wear Jane's. She was wearing one.'

Harry thought a moment. Slowly he said, 'It's too big for you. It'd slide around.'

Jamie looked desperate. His very existence, one felt, rested on the materialization of a crash helmet.

Brian stirred himself. 'He could wear a woolly hat underneath, stop it slipping about.' His expression said: if this lout has to turn up here and eat our food and show off his stomach muscles and steal our kids we might as well get something out of it in return.

Harry looked at Berry but she was concentrating on Zoe, refusing to be drawn into it. He turned back to Brian. 'If you say so,' he said. The inescapable translation being: it's your kid, if you want to risk it.

Jamie bounced up and down, knowing he'd won, and Brian scowled, clearly feeling he'd been manoeuvred into an irresponsible position. I thought Harry was being gratuitously unpleasant. He and I both knew he was a good enough driver not to throw Jamie off under the first passing car, and even if he was technically right to be cautious it seemed a lot of fuss for once round the block. Then it occurred to me that if Harry had suggested the ride, or agreed to the request immediately, Brian would have been the one to object; I suddenly guessed that Harry had anticipated this, and reacted in the only way likely to secure Brian's approval. I sighed inwardly. It was years since I had seen Brian so prickly, and Machiavellian moves and counter-moves made me very tired.

The ride thus tortuously agreed, we decamped to the front drive. Harry donned his leather jacket and gloves and re-stored Zoe's good humour by allowing her to painstakingly refasten all the boot buckles she had undone on the lawn. Jamie found the delay unbearable and jiggled around every-one exhaustingly, until Harry told him to stop being a wally and sent him inside for his snorkel coat. Berry then produced two woolly hats, one for Jamie's head and the other to stuff into the crown of Ruth's helmet. When they had finished with him the transmogrification was extraordinary: from small boy to freakish insect, top-heavy, shiny and alien.

Harry wheeled the bike on to the road, kicked it up and roared the engine for a few seconds, making Brian glance over his shoulder to see if the neighbours were watching, and Berry frown apprehensively. Jamie climbed on and wrapped his arms firmly round Harry's waist. It was almost an anticlimax when the engine note dropped to its normal rumble and the bike moved off at a sedate crawl down the road. Perhaps I was being unfair but I did wonder whether Harry hadn't created this contrast deliberately to discomfort Brian, a turn-of-the-screw reminder that while it was Brian who had encouraged his son to do something not quite correct, it was to himself as driver that he was being forced to entrust the responsibility.

They reappeared a minute later from the opposite direction – poor Berry, I'm sure she trusted Jamie not to fall off, but her face was still frozen all the time they were gone – and trundled towards us at the same restrained speed. As they pulled up Jamie joggled on the seat, as if the bike were a horse, and he was willing it to go faster.

Harry lifted his visor. 'What about Zoe?'

Brian was already shaking his head but Berry, holding Zoe's hand, can't have noticed. She looked down and the child's expression of unhoped-for delight made her reply super-fluous.

'If you like, darling,' Berry said, before Brian had a chance to verbally veto the idea. She helped Jamie dismount, exchanged the coat and helmet, and lifted Zoe aboard. The child clung to Harry's back with the whole of her body, twisting her great helmeted head away from us. Brian folded his arms and maintained a disapproving silence. At the last moment Berry bent over Zoe anxiously and said, 'You're sure now, darling, aren't you?'

The head nodded urgently. Berry stepped back and, as the bike pulled away, put a hand to her mouth. Brian's features were stiff with annoyance. The machinations of my brother-in-law's mind where his daughter is concerned is an enigma I've long since given up trying to understand.

The wait seemed longer this time. I felt the muscles in my own face tense, and then relax as the bike re-emerged into view.

Berry cried, 'Wasn't that fun?' as they drew up, her voice gay with relief.

Zoe apparently believed speech impossible within a helmet, and could only nod frantically as she scrambled off. Harry removed the impediment, releasing a babble of excitement, then tossed the woolly contents to Jamie and clipped the helmet on to the rack behind him. He regarded us all.

'OK?' he said. 'Rides over?'

I experienced a mischievous desire to hear Berry say, 'Me too, please,' and see Brian's reaction; she didn't, of course. Instead she shook her head definitely at Jamie, clutched both children's shoulders, and tugged them back a pace.

'Thanks for the lift,' I said.

'Right,' said Harry. 'Seeya.' He stepped on the gear lever, tipped his head to us, and pulled away. I suppose the lie of the road must by now have been extremely familiar to him, and of course he had no passenger to consider; as he disappeared round the first bend he was leaning in so far we all saw the rear footrest flick off the tarmac into the folded position.

Berry laughed at Jamie's frustrated expression, took Brian's arm in a conciliatory gesture, and led the way into the house.

Brian's jealousy of Harry – and Berry was right, he was jealous, you could tell from the belligerent way he asked about him later, as if looking for something he could be marked down on – I thought most unfair. And although part of it was circumstance – Harry's arrival with me and Brian's preconceived ideas and disillusion – it wasn't just that. He was jealous of the person Harry actually was, not of the person he suspected him to be. If Harry had turned out to be, say, a hippyish type, pursuing some gently alternative life-style from idealistic principles which set their own rules and standards, Brian's reaction would have been quite different, I was sure, whatever confusions had arisen to begin with. Once they had been dealt with he would have been happy to write him off as a wimp or crank, and certainly wouldn't have allowed any such (in his view) immature or freakish outlook to dent his own self-esteem.

But of course Harry wasn't like that. What Brian saw in Harry was someone who was quite simply and selfishly living a life doing exactly as he pleased, unfettered by causes, responsibilities or duties, and to Brian such indifferent and arrogant individualism was unforgivable. Everything about him became enviable: his apparent youth (even though Brian himself was not then thirty-six), his flat stomach, his glamorous appeal where the children were concerned, and perhaps also his reserve, as evidence of a lack of need for the approval, or even society, of others. But above all he envied Harry his freedom, both of action and philosophy, a freedom epitomized – if I was right to translate explicit disapproval into implicit jealousy – by the bike. And, although Harry was indeed freer than Brian, the jealousy was still unfair. Brian was himself extremely privileged. Unlike many others less fortunate, he had made his own choices about the type of life he led. He had no elderly relatives to look after, nobody had tricked him into marriage or forced unwanted children on him, or strapped him down and poured beer down his throat. He had chosen his own career and liked the money and status it gave him – neither of which Harry had – so that in effect he was jealous of Harry for the very things he himself had willingly foregone. Perhaps it was because Harry gave the impression of not wanting these things that devalued them in Brian's eyes, but they were still his choices and no one can have his cake and eat it too. And Brian had children, who unless he was extraordinarily unlucky he would have for the rest of his life, and Harry did openly value them, because he wanted children too; and yet Brian resented sharing them with him for just a few hours.

Harry couldn't win with someone like Brian, and maybe he'd worked that out before I had.

## Chapter 10

Berry was right about Brian, but wrong about Harry. Well, right and wrong. Right that he could drive a car ('You lied!' I accused him; 'Yup,' he nodded, unperturbed), but wrong about his looks. She may have seen him as deeply attractive but it must have been his type, or what he represented, that so impressed her, and not that he was really especially good looking – like Chris, say – because he wasn't. If he had been, I would have noticed. Once he became a friend I did like his face, and certainly his smile – a true reward, breaking from features so unpromising – but I like all my friends' faces, and smiles are nearly always a pleasure. Harry's looks were too hard to be properly handsome; although he must have been a couple of inches shorter than Chris his solidity made him look as if there might actually have been more of him, if it hadn't been packed into something so tough and ungiving. And his face under that uncompromising haircut almost never looked open or animated, which would have made it much more attractive.

But Berry wasn't completely wrong, because one night I did see him as new again, and, because he was dressed in what for him constituted fancy dress, he had let himself become someone quite different (rather as I felt on his bike, released from myself) and the result was spectacular.

It was the night I brought the Apple computer home from work, the first Friday in June. A venture born of guilt: it was now months since that afternoon I had missed our introduction to wordprocessors and stumbled across Harry drunk: the machine was there in the office and I was too scared to use it, but didn't want to be associated with all the other lecturers and secretaries who had been to the session and were still terrified of it. (Some of the lecturers – especially the men – were ridiculously head-in-the-sand about any machinery in the office. The photocopier had a large notice above it stating 'This is an equal opportunities copier', a hint from the all-female secretarial staff that they resented lecturers dumping work on them that with a moment's glance at the instructions they could just as easily have done themselves.)

But I was determined not to be left behind in the Processing Age (a Communication Skill after all, as my students were bound sooner or later to point out). What I needed, however, was time alone with the computer, and this was impossible in working hours. So I suggested to my Head of Department that if I had the chance to use it over the weekend I would return a more useful lecturer, and because he was one of those who attended the introduction and was still terrified, but needed people around him who weren't, he told me I could take it. (This was highly irregular, of course, but common practice with other college equipment; a Saturday night VCR burglar, for instance, would have been making a completely wasted trip.)

I cornered the department know-all for tips on setting the computer up, watched one of the secretaries at work on it, and when Friday afternoon came took several deep breaths and rang for a taxi to transport it home. While I waited for the taxi to arrive I contemplated my burden with foreboding – the casing plastic looked worryingly familiar, they probably made those crunching children's toys from the offcuts – and almost abandoned the idea; I might have, if I hadn't told

Harry I was bringing it home and promised him a session on it.

The worst part was carrying it from the taxi to the flat. I was convinced I was going to drop it outside the entrance as I wrestled with the doors, a disaster that had happened to Berry once with a bottle of red wine she'd carried all the way back from Italy for me.

However, I made it safely upstairs, through the lesser obstacle of my front door, and into the flat. I placed it in a corner of the sitting room away from telephones and hi-fi speakers as I had been told, made a second trip to bring up the manual and diskettes and my shopping, and then with my confidence renewed – using the thing must be child's play compared to not dropping it – ran downstairs to tell the others it had arrived.

'It's here!' I was going to say. But the view, as the door swung wide, erased all computing thoughts. Before me, a darkly immaculate arm outstretched to the latch, stood a vision of elegance: Harry, just recognizable, in bow tie and dinner suit.

I had known they were going out – it was why I had called down early – but not what a major event it was clearly to be. Since I couldn't disguise my amazement I was forced to make a joke out of it.

'My God, Harry!' I said, raising a hand to my forehead as if scanning the horizon. 'Is that you in there?'

He waved me in with a grin, looking every bit as impressed as I was by the transformation. It wasn't really the dinner suit – they're really rather dull and uniform-like – but more the whole change of image, and the way it seemed to have affected the person inside.

'Wow,' I said, circling him slowly. 'You look stunning!'

He mooched shamelessly around in front of the hall mirror practising looking dignified and stunning for a few seconds.

Then dug his hands in his pockets and said, 'Ruth isn't wearing her glasses tonight. I'm playing guide dog,' as if impelled to explain why he was accompanying her on such an out-of-character mission.

Ruth's voice from the bedroom called, 'Don't believe a word he says, he's as high as a kite.'

He was; I'd never seen him so alive and outgoing. He was clearly delighted with his appearance, though not in a vain way, more as if he was admiring someone else entirely. He offered me a drink, which I accepted, and ran around playing the perfect host and being altogether unHarry-like. I did wonder if this unusual animation was alcohol-assisted, but I don't think it was; I think he was one of those individuals who, if conditions are to their liking, can get high on circumstance and atmosphere. They were going as guests of a grateful client to a stuffy banquet that would be peopled with minor politicians and other worthies, none of whom he would have anything in common with. But he had simply decided he was going to have some fun and had worked himself into a frame of mind that would be entertained by such a pompous event.

After a while Ruth emerged from the bedroom. She looked pretty good too, in a long green dress with no back, her hair, hennaed auburn, piled high on her head, and without her glasses. Not that she doesn't look attractive in glasses, but they never seem to go with long dresses.

Harry became quite gallant – he could make the right moves, I realized, when he chose – and kissed her hand. Ruth actually blushed. I was astounded that after six years living together he could have this effect on her. Or maybe dressed like that and in such a mood he was a stranger to her too, and that was why.

I raised my glass and complimented them both on their appearances.

'Yes, he looks fantastic, doesn't he?' Ruth said, very unpatronizingly, and they exchanged glances that caused me a moment's pain. Only a moment's; the pain is much worse now, thinking back, and I don't believe I was jealous, but I do remember saying to myself: these are my friends, these two, and I'm going to know them all my life if they'll let me. Friends are more durable than lovers, in my experience, and I've always taken a lot of trouble with them. And I tried to imagine what we would all be like twenty years on, when I would be fifty-seven, and Ruth fifty-two, and Harry forty-eight, and what we would all be doing: I had enough difficulty with myself and Ruth, but with Harry I couldn't get anywhere at all.

Then we topped up our glasses and the atmosphere became more partylike. Ruth told me, grinning, that she had had to persuade Harry out of adding a jarring note to his appearance by biroing LOVE and HATE tattoos on his knuckles, and had only succeeded by convincing him that most of the other guests were East End gangsters gone legit, who wouldn't be in the least disconcerted.

I told Harry airily (and rather impertinently, thinking back) that given his fondness for hazardous experiences I was surprised he didn't have any genuine tattoos to flaunt.

'Well,' he said carefully, 'not on my hands.'

'Oh,' I said, deservedly thrown. I couldn't tell if he was teasing.

'They hurt, you know,' he added ambiguously; which I was left to interpret, amid Ruth's snorts of unenlightening laughter, as I pleased.

Their taxi arrived soon afterwards and I went back upstairs. I had intended to ring Chris and suggest he came round after I'd set the computer up and played with it a while; but I never made the call. I told myself I was having one of my luxurious solitary evenings instead, only it wasn't as enjoyable as they usually were. I ended up watching the late film on television, which wasn't worth it but put off the moment of going to bed, so that when I finally switched off the light I had only a few minutes alone with myself in the darkness before my thoughts were drowned by sleep.

It was the next day that things started to go wrong. It was Brian's fault, really, and he should have known better, but he didn't do it deliberately; it was only thoughtlessness and gullibility, and very likely it would have happened anyway, somehow or other. He felt dreadful about it afterwards and I at least have forgiven him, even if I've never forgiven myself. Because it was a mistake anyone could make when they're busy and not on the ball.

I had a visitor to my flat at about four-thirty on the Saturday afternoon. Harry and I were in the sitting room, changing background colours on the computer monitor: hardly a demanding exercise, but quite fun. We'd had a session with the Wordstar disk but without a printer we couldn't do anything permanent, and Harry was more interested in graphics anyway, so this was a kind of pre-liminary foray.

For a beginner Harry was very bold with the computer. I worried that something catastrophic would happen if I typed in the wrong word or pressed the wrong key, but he said 'Rubbish' and invoked just the atmosphere to make the computer understand that we were the masters and it the slave; and indeed nothing did happen except blank screens and 'Syntax Error'. The only caution I insisted he grasp was to on no account turn the computer off with the disks inserted; the thought of wiping out a dubiously borrowed Wordstar, and having to explain to the office staff on Monday where and why it had gone, loomed large in my mind.

When the doorbell rang I was typing in codes, so Harry went to answer it. I heard a male voice say something that could have been, 'Who are you?' and Harry's voice, louder, saying in return, 'What's it to you?'

Christ, I thought, scraping my chair back, now he's being rude to some friend of mine who's called round.

I hurried through to the hall. But the visitor was a stranger to me, a smooth-faced man in his forties with thinning slicked-back hair and wearing a suit and tie, though still looking the shabby side of smart: an overworked small-business man, perhaps, or minor council official. I couldn't understand why Harry was regarding him so belligerently; there was only one of him, he wasn't a gang, which would have been more worth while antagonizing; and then I glanced at the man and saw that he was bristling too. I wondered who the hell had started this.

The man relaxed when he saw me – the reason for which I only understood later – and after I had dismissed the notion that he and Harry might know each other and have some history to sort out – it was my flat, after all – I pushed Harry aside and asked the man what he wanted.

In a courteous tone he asked if I was Miss Hardy.

I said I was.

'Oh good,' he nodded. 'I'm a probation officer. Trying to trace a Mrs Joanna Maskin. I've some news for her, about her husband.'

'He's lying,' said Harry immediately, making the atmosphere very tense again.

'Have you got identification?' I asked. I tried to say it

inoffensively, as any security-conscious citizen might, and blamed Harry, not the stranger at this point, for making it difficult.

The man opened his jacket and dug around in the inside pockets. He looked perplexed, then seemed to remember something and touched his forehead. 'It's in the office. Oh dear. So silly. I do apologize.'

Although he said it plausibly I couldn't believe him. I started to feel nervous: of a scene, of how he had got my address, and behind both – though as yet dimly, because of my mind's reluctance to dwell on it – of who he himself must be. But I wasn't frightened; after that first flash with Harry he had become mild and soft-spoken, he wasn't an enormous thug of a man, and anyway I had Harry with me.

'Mrs Maskin does live here, doesn't she?' the man asked.

'No,' I replied quickly; too quickly, because what I should have done, right from the start, before even asking for his card, was deny I knew Joanna at all. But you only think of these things afterwards.

He gave me a brief, registering smile. 'Do you know where I can find her?'

'No,' I said again, but this time not fast enough, and I knew he'd guessed I was lying. Although it was possible I wasn't; I remembered Joanna's hints last September about moving on. But though my hesitancy was caused as much by uncertainty as by a decision to lie, the effect was the same.

There was an uncomfortable silence. He looked reluctant to leave matters at that, and I didn't know how to get rid of him politely. Somehow I couldn't bring myself to explode the civilized charade as long as he was still maintaining it.

'I think you'd better go,' Harry said finally; they exchanged glances, not very pleasant ones, and the man left.

I banged the front door shut and rushed to the sitting room

window, to make sure he was really leaving. Harry came up behind me. We saw the man as he emerged from the flats; he turned to walk along the road below us and, as he passed, lifted his eyes towards us.

I pulled back, embarrassed, but Harry didn't. If he'd been Chris I'd have whispered an excruciated 'Don't!' and yanked him away; as it was I grimaced the word urgently, but silently, at Harry's back.

Eventually he turned round and said, 'How the hell did he know to come here?'

'He's gone now, has he?' I asked.

'Yup.'

I thought a moment, and then because it was the obvious starting point, said, 'I think I'd better ring Berry.'

'Yeah,' nodded Harry, 'I think you'd better.'

I returned to the hall for the phone and when I got through tried not to sound too alarmist. 'I think,' I said, after we'd exchanged greetings, 'that I've just had a visit from Joanna's husband.'

'My God!' Berry exclaimed, and then immediately protested, 'But you can't have, he's in prison.'

'I don't think he is,' I said; and when we worked out the dates, taking remission into account, she agreed he probably wasn't.

'But how could he have got your address?' Behind her indignant tone I could hear her brain working frantically, checking and rechecking her own innocence.

I said I didn't know, and that was why I was ringing her. I gave her a word-for-word replay of the doorstep conversation, and she sounded baffled at first, but then suddenly interrupted with a flustered, 'Wait. Jane . . . hang on . . .'

I heard a muffled voice in the background and then she said Brian wanted to tell her something, and she'd ring me back.

I put the receiver down and waited in the sitting room doorway, gnawing a thumb nail. Harry was still over by the window, staring out, as if hoping to catch the man creeping back.

When the phone rang I snatched it up and it was Berry again, sounding angry and distressed. She said my caller had got the address from Brian. A man had called at the house the previous evening, while he was in the front garden trying to persuade the children to bring in their bikes and go to bed. She had been out at a CND meeting. The man had said he was a probation officer and it had never occurred to Brian to doubt it, because he had looked like one (whatever that meant). And he hadn't given him my address, because the man hadn't asked for it. The man had said merely that he wanted to trace Joanna to pass on a message from the prison service, and Brian had assumed something had happened to Joanna's husband in prison and said, 'Well, you could try my sister-in-law,' and given him my name and telephone number. But of course I was in the phone book, so the rest would have been easy. I spoke to Brian and asked him to describe the man, and it had to be the same one.

'Sorry,' he sighed at the end, sounding wearily apologetic.

I was distracted and needed time – and Ruth, I suddenly realized – to work out the implications. I told him it didn't matter, it was done now, and we'd sort it out our end.

'Is Ruth in?' I asked Harry as I put the phone down.

'Yes.' He nodded, as if following my train of thought. 'You'd better come downstairs.'

Ruth was hot-oiling her hair, but it was already wrapped in a towel and she seemed unfazed by the interruption. She pulled on a dressing gown over her jeans and bra and joined us in the sitting room.

Harry explained what had happened. It seemed like a game at first, or unreal enough to discuss like a game. We all agreed my caller had been Maskin. (His first name was George. But we stuck to Maskin.) We debated calling the police.

'It must be a crime,' I said. 'Pretending to be a probation officer. Deception. I don't know.' It was me Maskin had called on, he was a bad person, and it was the police's job to deal with bad people. That's what I meant.

'They won't be interested,' Harry said contemptuously. 'Waste of time.'

Ruth was carefully neutral.

'I don't think he's committed much of an offence, Jane,' she warned me. 'Not by just verbally pretending to be a probation officer. He was quite clever really, not having a card. And he was only trying to deceive you out of information, and, from the police point of view, pretty mundane information.'

She wanted to know which prison he'd been held in.

I thought and with sudden shame said, 'I don't know.' How could I have lived with Joanna all that time and not known? Had we ever really talked?

But if Ruth thought my confession odd she didn't let on. She just said, 'Pity. I wonder if he's genuinely released or on parole. If he's still on parole it'd be more sensible to contact his parole officer rather than the police. When did he go to prison?'

Berry and I had just calculated this. 'Nineteen months ago.'

Ruth pulled a face. 'It was only a two-year sentence, wasn't it? He must have been out a while. He won't be on parole. Damn.'

'He lied, though,' I insisted. 'And he's trying to find Joanna . . .'

'Yeah,' said Harry. 'Somewhere in London there's an ex-con who's lied trying to find his ex-wife. The police'll mount a manhunt.'

'All right,' I said testily. 'So what do I do?'

'Tell Joanna,' said Ruth.

'Oh God,' I said.

'You've got to,' said Ruth. 'He might get her address somewhere else. You've got to warn her.'

I sighed. 'You don't think he does just want to speak to her?'

'Doesn't matter,' said Ruth. 'She's got to know.'

I knew Ruth was right but I was deeply reluctant. It was going to be so frightening for Joanna, after nearly two years of a new, safe life, to be told he was looking for her. She wouldn't know his motives any more than we did, but I knew what she would assume. Even if he never found her she was going to suffer.

And yet it would be even worse if he got her address elsewhere and we hadn't warned her.

In the end, as she wasn't on the telephone, we decided I should write her a note. Ruth gave me a pencil and paper and we roughed it out. I'd give Joanna the facts but present them as unfrighteningly as possible. Just say Maskin had called, claiming he had news for her, had seemed calm and polite, but that of course we had said we'd no idea where she was, and that he had left and we didn't expect to see him again. (Which wasn't altogether true, as transpired later, but seemed to close the episode reassuringly.) I would also recommend that if there were any other links to her old life she might want to remind them not to reveal her address. We decided not to say Maskin had pretended to be someone else; we felt the letter read ominously enough without that. And finally I would add – just as a PS, to show how unlikely I thought it – that if by any chance she did want to see him then to ring me, and if I happened to see him again I'd tell him. I'd send the note to the Archway address and if she was still there she would be alerted, but not, we hoped, unduly frightened; and if she had moved on she wouldn't get the warning but she was probably safe anyway, and we would have done our best.

That settled, we turned to the question of what Maskin was likely to do now and, in particular, whether there was a chance he might turn up at the flats again.

'Depends whether he gets lucky somewhere else,' Harry said.

'You mean if he doesn't he'll be back?' I asked.

Harry shrugged.

Ruth asked, 'Do you know anyone else – perhaps in Norwich – he could try? Other womenfriends, or relatives? Has your sister got Joanna's address?'

'I don't know,' I said. 'I don't think so. Not from me. The whole point was to cut ties . . .'

'He's tried Norwich,' Harry said. 'That's why he's here. You're all he got.'

I suspected he was right, and I could see Ruth did too. Cautiously she asked if I might have left Maskin with the impression that I did know where Joanna was.

'I think,' I said, 'that we should work on that assumption.'

Harry gave me a scornful look and said that it would have been obvious to an idiot that I was lying.

Ruth digested this and then said, 'Well, what sort of person is he? I know he's been violent to his wife . . . but how is he with other people?'

This question rattled me a little, though the more I thought about it the more reassured I was. I didn't know much about Maskin, but I did know that one of the reasons he never received much official retribution for what he did to Joanna was because he had always seemed such a rational and mild-mannered man in public. He had come across as the saner of the two in court (because Joanna was terrified witless and he wasn't) and he had had no past record of violence. This meant that he had been convicted more in sorrow than anger, incurring remarks from the bench about how 'even if you are provoked (the implication being that Joanna's behaviour must have been provocative to arouse violence in such a reasonable man), you have a duty not to break the law and inflict physical injury on your wife'. So although he was found guilty and even briefly sent down on one occasion, the moral victory had been his, and she was soon discouraged from using the law at all.

'It's amazing, isn't it,' I finished, 'that a man can be like that? I mean non-violent in his public life but vicious to his wife at home. Don't you think it's extraordinary?'

Ruth shook her head. 'Not really. Lots of men treat their wives as non-persons that the normal rules of decency don't apply to. They think their wives belong to them, so they've got a right to punish them. The same isn't true for outsiders. In fact I've heard some women say their husbands were really chivalrous towards them when they were courting. They didn't become tyrants until they got married. The women thought it must be their fault, but of course it wasn't. It was because of how their husbands viewed their rights in marriage.'

I found this interesting and would have liked to pursue it further, but Harry had recognized the signs of incipient intellectualism and was becoming restless. A shame, I thought, as the moment passed. I'd never before had the chance to discuss violence in the company of a man who, to my certain knowledge, had both given and received it.

However, Ruth's words were personally cheering, since the type she described seemed to approximate to the little we knew about Maskin. Of course we didn't know what prison might have done to him, but, as Ruth said, it was worth remembering that he was out to find Joanna, not me. If his motives were innocent then there was no reason to suppose he would behave violently to effect them, and if they weren't, and he was vindictive enough to want to hurt her after all this time, he was unlikely to spoil his chances by getting arrested for assaulting someone else.

Ruth had a heartening, competent approach to the whole matter. She enquired logically after the facts, few as they were, hypothesized convincingly on courses of action – both ours and Maskin's – and advised lucidly on the likely results. I reckoned she must be very good at her job and almost wished Maskin was with us to hear it as well, and give in with good grace once he knew what his options were, and what he was up against. She made just one recommendation: not to go to the police this time but to definitely involve them if Maskin turned up again, however reasonable he seemed, as much to be able to warn him we were going to, and mean it, as for what they would be able to do.

I asked her if, personally, she thought he'd come back.

'God knows,' she said, screwing up her nose. 'Depends how desperate he is.'

Of course, she hadn't met him. I myself was confused as to what I thought. To me Maskin had been polite and inoffensive, even if he had lied. And though I knew what he had done to Joanna, knew it intellectually, I also knew that I hadn't, as I would have expected, been frightened of him. He hadn't come across as brutish or intimidating, and to be honest, the facts were difficult to associate with the man. Without foreknowledge, based purely on his appearance and manner, I would have described him as pathetic, not dangerous.

But, on the other hand, it was clear that Harry had mistrusted him from the start and because I respected Harry's intuitions by now I was influenced by this. I was prepared to take his word that Maskin had been looking for trouble with his 'Who are you?' when he first arrived, and it occurred to both of us that if Maskin believed Joanna still lived in the flat he might have seen Harry as a boyfriend. Harry claimed to have picked up an immediate hostility.

He said he wouldn't trust Maskin an inch, that anyone could see he was a nasty piece of work whatever manners he could turn on when it suited him, and he wished now he'd given him more of a warning about the welcome he could expect if he showed up again.

At this Ruth rolled her eyes and said there was nothing to be gained by stirring up trouble where none might otherwise exist, and at the time – way into supperless evening by now, with nothing but whisky and wine to sustain us – I rather agreed.

# Chapter 11

I wrote my note to Joanna and posted it on the Sunday, and both Ruth and Harry spent a lot of time that day in my flat playing with the computer; which may have been out of genuine interest, or may have been them being neighbourly. But if it was the latter their chaperonage was wasted, because nothing untoward occurred; I had only one caller, a squeaky-clean little Jehovah's Witness, who made a hesitant attempt to convert Harry, and left much sooner than they do when it's me on my own.

I didn't tell Chris what had happened till Monday, when I saw him at work. I hadn't rung him over the weekend; I thought it would only result in him worrying impotently – he had had his daughters with him on the Sunday and couldn't have come rushing over.

I told him during our morning coffee break and he looked so shocked I found myself down-playing the incident. At the end of the account he took my hand.

'Of course you're anxious,' he said. 'Anyone would be. It's only natural. D'you want to get away? My house is yours, anytime, you know it is.'

'Oh, no,' I said. 'It's not that bad. And Joanna might ring. But thanks.' I was grateful. He hadn't liked Joanna, and I'd somehow thought this would have led to him underrating her side of the story. Particularly since he had only got it second-

hand, and with what he might have seen as female partisanship, from me. But I'd misjudged him.

'Well,' he said. 'D'you want company at your place, just till
it's sorted out? You've only got to say.'

'No,' I said. 'Honestly. I'm really not that nervous.' I wasn't
– looked at objectively and in the company of others there
seemed very little to be nervous about.

'But thanks,' I said warmly. 'I really do appreciate the offer.'

He smiled. 'Anything you say. You change your mind, let
me know.'

'I will,' I said, and felt more affectionate towards him than I
had for weeks.

On Tuesday evening I had a visit from the police. As I opened
the door to the uniforms I automatically assumed it would
have something to do with Maskin – an indication of how my
mind was running, I suppose, even if I wasn't worrying – but I
was wrong. They'd come as errand boys. One was holding a
battered plastic object that on inspection proved to be – or have
been, rather – my cassette player, the one that was stolen.

My first reaction was: oh God no, that's what comes of
being efficient and keeping serial numbers, thinking of the
vastly superior trouble-free machine I'd bought with the
insurance money; but when I cautiously enquired, the policemen smiled and said they didn't think the insurance company
necessarily needed to know, as it had all happened such a long
time ago, and the thing was so clearly the worse for wear.

Harry had been right, it turned out; my burglars were kids,
two boys in their teens. The officers said they had been picked
up for something quite different (unspecified) but the cassette
player had been found among their effects, along with a horde
of other stolen goods – though sadly not my jewellery –
which, where ownership could be established, the police were

now distributing. I felt slightly sorry for the officers, imagining dozens of recipients like myself, cursing the return of untreasured and long-replaced possessions.

When they had gone I took the player into the sitting room, and, curious to see if anything on it did still work, pressed the eject button. Inside the cavity I found the remains of an ancient sandwich; I couldn't imagine what had prompted anyone to do something so bizarre. A minute later Ruth came up, anxious to know what the police had wanted (it was suddenly very comforting to know I had friends so close who weren't afraid of appearing nosy). I showed her the sandwich and in a mood of relieved hilarity we speculated on various scenarios, finally deciding that the boys had discovered the player's proclivity for chewing up tapes, and in the hope of reducing its hunger had tried to satisfy it with a sandwich instead.

I didn't fancy picking out the bits, and doubted it would work even if I did, so after admiring it a while I disposed of it in the dustbin; where it could eat what it liked, for all I cared.

Maskin didn't turn up again till the Thursday. And he picked his moment with care. Of course he can't have known how Harry fitted in: whether he was a friend visiting or someone I lived with, so very likely he had checked the place out earlier. Then he only had to settle himself somewhere unobtrusive to be sure of catching me as I returned from work.

It was a suffocatingly hot afternoon (exams were in full spate at college, precipitating the usual heatwave) and I dripped my way up to the flat laden with work bags, dumped them in the study, and returned to the hall to close the front door. And there was Maskin – in the same suit and tie as Saturday, defying the temperature – standing on the doorstep. Just inside the doorstep actually; the only thing that stopped me banging the door shut on him was the thought that if I did he might lose a toe.

He must have seen from my face what an unwelcome visitor he was.

'About Saturday . . .' he said quickly. 'I just wanted to apologize . . .' His features puckered to an expression of self-deprecation. 'So silly . . . obviously you didn't believe me . . . only it's very important I see my wife . . . er, Joanna.' He smiled at me sadly. 'You understand it's difficult in the . . . um . . . circumstances. I didn't know what attitude . . .' His shoulders lifted helplessly. 'Some people, well . . . er . . .' He gathered breath and continued more bravely. 'It really is vital I see her. A lot of things to discuss. You . . . um . . . I'm sure you understand . . .'

I wondered whether he meant by the 'um . . . circumstances' being a former convict, or a former wife-beater. I had also noted his use of 'wife', when referring to Joanna, and not 'ex-wife'. These thoughts should have added to my apprehension, but in fact his cringingly obsequious manner was in danger of undermining it altogether. So much so that I was even tempted to enquire after these supposedly vital communications, and only didn't because I thought it might unfairly encourage him.

However, the atmosphere at least felt more honest.

'But Joanna doesn't want to see you,' I said. I could no longer bring myself to pretend complete ignorance. 'I'm sorry, but I know she doesn't.'

'Has she told you that?' He looked distressed. 'Does she know I want to see her?'

I hesitated. I couldn't tell from his expression – eager now as well as anxious – if he knew he was being clever.

'Look,' I said, rather regretting sparing the toe, 'I know she doesn't want to see you, and I think you know it too. It's why she moved here in the first place, isn't it? She doesn't actually know you're looking for her, at least not from me, because I don't know where she is. It's eighteen months since she left. But if she had changed her mind she's had plenty of time to contact you, and if you haven't heard from her I would think it means she hasn't. I'm sorry.'

He lowered his gaze and frowned over this. I kicked myself for the second 'I'm sorry' and wished conflict didn't always arouse in me the drivelling urge to apologize. But the rest, I thought, had sounded OK. Even the lie about Joanna's whereabouts sounded moderately credible, buried amongst the truth like that.

He lifted his eyes to mine hopefully. 'I could write her a letter. Ask her if she'd see me.'

'No, you couldn't,' I said. 'You haven't got her address.'

There was a moment's eyelocked impasse. He shifted position. 'Could I leave it with you?' he asked wheedlingly. 'Perhaps . . .'

'But I haven't got it either,' I said steadily. 'I just told you.'

'Oh yes,' he nodded. 'Silly of me.'

I felt myself flush. 'Will you go now, please,' I said. 'I'm very busy.'

He nodded again, but absently. He seemed to have lost interest in the conversation. He was staring over my shoulder, into the flat. Feeling oddly invisible, I watched his eyes roam.

I remembered, with a lurch of alarm, that my address book was lying on the hall table next to the telephone. It wasn't very obviously an address book, because over the years it had disintegrated and been reborn under red vinyl. But it was there, nevertheless, and to those wandering eyes, I was suddenly convinced, frighteningly exposed.

Maskin picked up the change in mood immediately. His eyes flicked from the flat to me and with renewed intensity – as if now certain there was something worth looking for – back to the flat again. I felt like someone tricked into a game of I Spy, and, sinkingly, that I had just signalled 'getting warm'.

I cleared my throat. 'You'll have to go,' I said, and managed this time to swallow the 'I'm sorry'. I put my hand on the latch and started to close the door.

Without breaking his gaze Maskin lifted his own arm and casually – and quite unthreateningly – steadied it. He gave me a fleeting blank smile, stepped sideways – exactly as if we had just met in the doorway, and he was graciously letting me pass – and was suddenly behind me, inside the flat.

'Excuse me!' I protested. I meant to convey outrage, but my voice came out as a feeble squeak. I'd lost control. He took several steps into the hall and stopped between the table and sitting room door. Not yet homed in on the address book, but horribly close. Too close for surreptitious manoeuvres; or even a dash to snatch it up, if I wanted to be sure of escape.

I couldn't think what to do. I babbled, 'Please go, will you, please go,' several times, without effect. I could have been inaudible, as well as invisible. He was right beside the table now, even closer to the address book, though mercifully peering the wrong way, into the sitting room.

A surge of anger made me take a step towards him, before the realization struck me – so forcibly it seemed to make the room judder – that I was standing within an arm's length of, and in direct conflict with, a man who had once kicked a fallen woman in the mouth so hard he had broken her jaw.

I turned, and did the only thing I could think of doing, which was to hurtle downstairs for help.

Harry was in, but had been asleep, which meant he took longer than usual to answer the door. And when he did I was startled to see that he was wearing only a pair of black underpants, very skimpy ones at that. He probably hadn't even been wearing them when I knocked, judging from the way he was still adjusting them.

'He's in my flat!' I gasped. 'Maskin! The door was open and he just walked in! I can't get rid of him.'

Harry blinked at me.

'Maskin,' I repeated urgently. 'Upstairs.'

'Right,' he said. He rubbed his face, and, as if an inner motor had been sparked into life, looked instantly ready for action. He grasped my wrist and tugged me through the doorway of the flat.

'You stay there,' he ordered, moving to the stairs. 'And close the door!' He bounded upwards.

I obeyed the first command, but not the second. It would have been too wet. Also, though I didn't seriously doubt Harry could deal with Maskin, I wanted to witness him dealt with, to be quite sure.

Within thirty seconds the two appeared on the stairs, preceded by the sounds of argument, belligerent on Harry's part, plaintive on Maskin's. Astonishingly – and exciting in me undaredfor hopes – Maskin was still wailing on about his need for our help. They made the most incongruous-looking pair. Usually lack of clothes makes people appear vulnerable and at a disadvantage, and given Maskin's suit and tie the discrepancy should have been pronounced. But there was in fact no question as to who had the upper hand, and I had never, observing Harry's display of self-confidently righteous aggression, seen a virtually naked man look less vulnerable.

'And don't fucking show your face here again,' he said violently, as they approached the bottom of the stairs.

Maskin stumbled on the last step, making the verbal assault look physical.

I retreated – a nice cowardice, sparing Maskin's feelings along with my own – and crept out again when they had passed the flat door. In time to see Harry yank open one of the lobby doors, push Maskin outside, and bang it shut.

Maskin turned and started to say something through the glass. I couldn't catch the words, but it looked mournful.

'He's not going,' I said.

'Shit,' muttered Harry and slammed out after him. I heard him say irritably, 'You fucking push your luck, don't you?' He grasped Maskin by the arm, and marched him down the path to the pavement.

I moved to the lobby doors and through the glass watched them stand for a few moments arguing. Their voices were lost in the drone of the rush-hour traffic, but stance and gesture conveyed the gist. Even at this distance I could see small dangerous flexing movements in Harry's back; I thought how intimidating he looked, and realized how much language – unconscious, instinctive language – is normally hidden by clothes. When Maskin finally turned away he looked a disappointed man; but then his body was covered, and its signals hidden from us. The deceit would have been easy.

As soon as he had gone I raced for the stairs. Before the first landing I heard the crash of the lobby doors, and the pounding of feet below. I found myself praying that Mrs Rosen hadn't witnessed the pavement argument, and wasn't gleefully on her way round to investigate. And inconsequently from that, in the way trivia insists on infiltrating the most desperate thoughts, that I now knew Harry had no tattoos, unless they were tiny, and very intimately placed.

From the front door of my flat I could see that the address

book had been moved. I ran to it and snatched it up, with a last-ditch hope that he might not have spotted her name; I'd had the book for years and it contained hundreds of entries, many crossed out to keep pace with moves. Moreover, I'd entered Joanna under J rather than M or P (for Pym, the maiden name she was reverting to) to save confusion.

But when I went through the book – God knows why, I must have thought I'd be able to tell from the page whether his eyes had been there – even that hope collapsed, because the whole of page J was simply missing. Perhaps he didn't trust his memory, or couldn't find a pen; or perhaps he just wanted to show us he'd won.

Harry arrived, scarcely breathless, beside me.

'Oh God,' I moaned, and showed him the book.

He swore and glanced over his shoulder, as if contemplating a pavement chase; then shrugged, dismissing it. Even if he had caught Maskin and forcibly removed the paper, nothing could alter the fact that he'd seen it.

I groaned, 'We must tell her,' and felt sick with guilt, because I knew I should have removed the entry myself, after the first visit. I could see Harry was thinking the same, but was being kind enough not to say it.

Unhappily I asked, 'D'you think he'll go round there straight away?'

'I would,' replied Harry. 'Wouldn't you?'

I stared at him. 'The police,' I said. 'We must tell the police.'

Harry shrugged again. 'If you like.' He sounded un-enthusiastic. 'What're you going to ask them to do? Run a message saying "Your ex-husband is coming to see you this evening, possibly"?'

'Oh God.' I rubbed at my forehead.

Harry smiled briefly. 'It's OK,' he said. 'I'll nip over on the bike and warn her. With any luck he won't have a car, and even if he's got the money he's not stupid enough to take a taxi, not if he's planning anything. It'll take him a while on the tube.'

'I'll have to come too,' I said quickly. It didn't cross my mind to refuse the offer. 'She'll have got my letter. She doesn't know you. She might think it's a trap.'

Harry shook his head. 'You can't. She might want a lift somewhere.' He moved to the door. 'Look, I'll get dressed. Write her a note . . . anything, just so she knows it's you. I'll explain when I get there.'

'Right.' I gave up trying to think. It only seemed to be slowing things down.

Harry disappeared. I ran into the study and scrabbled through the desk in the study for a sheet of college-headed writing paper, and in a triumph of will over vibration-power, wrote a desperately apologetic few words on to it. I finished with 'You can trust Harry absolutely,' instantly regretted it – his presence said as much, and he was bound to read it – but realized that having written it, I could hardly cross it out. I began a rewrite but was interrupted by the rumble of the bike starting up outside. I grabbed the original and tore downstairs.

Out the front I told him the address and handed him the note. I squirmed while he read it and muttered, 'Absolutely,' over it; and then he roared away with the spare helmet behind him, leaving me feeling I couldn't have made a bigger mess of things if I'd tried.

The rest of the evening seemed to last for ever.

Ruth arrived home only minutes after Harry had left, and after a garbled briefing I rang the police from her flat. I told them a man had pushed his way through my open front door and wandered round my hall, and they replied, 'Oh yes? Did he take anything?' and seemed underwhelmed with interest when I said he'd stolen a page from my address book. However, they did promise to send a constable round, and twenty minutes later, just as Ruth was telling me to sit down and relax, because he could be hours yet, a uniformed officer appeared at the open front door.

Ruth made mugs of tea and took us all through to the sitting room. Without his helmet the officer was revealed as blond and depressingly young. I couldn't imagine him having a marital status at all. When I'd finished telling him what had happened he frowned over his notebook and said they could probably get someone to pop round to Joanna's, just to check on her, but that he doubted Maskin could be picked up for more than a fatherly chat at this stage. Nosing about someone's flat in the middle of a conversation with the owner wasn't, it appeared, much of a crime; he'd made no menacing remarks to me, and the theft of one piece of paper, though technically an offence, seemed unlikely to be enough to warrant prosecution.

'But he could kill her!' I cried. 'Can't you arrest him for threatening behaviour or something?'

'Have you actually heard him threaten her?' He lifted his pen.

Well no, I admitted, but we all knew that's what he was doing.

He waggled the pen over the paper. With the air of someone trying to show willing, he asked, 'Would there be an injunction out against him, d'you know?'

'Well . . . I'm not sure.' I looked to Ruth for advice. I wasn't certain what an injunction was, beyond being a sort of court order. Though I thought they had figured in Joanna's past.

'No, there wouldn't,' Ruth said definitely. 'They'd have expired years ago.' She touched me on the arm. 'Leave it, Jane,' she said. 'They can't do anything. Not till he does something. It's always the same.'

The policeman stood up and tucked his notebook away in his breast pocket. 'If your friend is in serious danger,' he said, not looking at us, 'she'll get the same protection as anyone else.'

I stood up too, since the interview was obviously over. Walking to the front door to see him out I muttered, 'Some protection,' but only to myself, out of frustration, and I don't think he heard.

At half-past six Harry rang in from a phone box, having had the sense to try his own number after failing to raise me on mine. Ruth was changing out of sticky work clothes in the bedroom, so I answered it. The sound of his voice made a muscle at the bottom of my throat pulsate.

'Where are you?' I asked. 'Was she there?' Say no, I prayed.

'Yup,' he said.

'Oh God.'

'I got her here now, with some things.' His tone was neutral. 'We're at Alexandra Park. Outside a pub. She needs somewhere to go.'

'Oh God,' I said again. I pulled a desperate face at Ruth, just entering the sitting room. She pulled a chair up quietly and leant forward to listen.

'I said I'd wait at the bedsit with her,' Harry went on, '. . . but she said she wanted to go now. It makes sense. I can't stay for ever, and if she's going to have to move anyway she might as well get a head start.' His voice went faint and then returned, sounding hurried. 'Look . . . I haven't got much change. Ring me back.' He gave me the number and rang off.

I rang back. The phone was answered by a female 'Hello?', thin and strained.

'Joanna?' I was taken by surprise, and immediately felt the need to make my voice warm and reassuring. 'Hello, Joanna,' I said again. 'Harry says you need somewhere to go.'

'I can't stay in the bedsit.' Her voice was unresponsively remote. 'I don't want to go back there.'

'No,' I said. In my mind's eye I saw her face: bland and masklike, its character blotted out under the layers of make-up. I had only twice, in the months she stayed with me, seen her face naked. Berry said it was low self-esteem that made her do it.

'Do you want to come here?' I asked kindly. I assumed this was why they had telephoned. 'I mean, just till you find somewhere else?' I caught Ruth's eye, looking very dubious, and was suddenly confused.

There was a short silence the other end. Then I heard her say unsteadily, not to me, 'She says her flat . . . but he's been there . . .'

Harry's voice came on again, flat and definite. 'Your place's out. And ours. It has to be somewhere he doesn't know.'

'But . . .' I was at a loss. I didn't see how I was meant to solve it. Even, indignation forerunning panic, why I should be expected to. 'Hasn't she got any friends who'd put her up?' I could hear a whine creeping into my voice.

There was a clatter, and sounds of a conference again. Ruth whispered, 'I wouldn't bank on it. I don't expect she's told them.'

'Jane?' said Harry's voice, expressionless. 'No, she hasn't.'

I heard a clear 'don't push it'. Obstinately, I wanted to argue, 'It's nothing to be ashamed of, what are friends for?' but I didn't say it. I knew she was ashamed, and couldn't simply be told not to be. And anyway, that being the woman she was – or had been damaged into – she might not have too many friends.

I had just thought of Chris, and his house – he'd do it but hate being bullied into it, and, besides, it ought to be a woman – when I was distracted by the sight of Ruth's fingers, agitating in front of me.

'Jane,' she whispered, 'Let me speak to him. I've done this before.'

It took me a moment to believe she was offering to take over. I checked with her face, and silently handed her the receiver. Even the way she tucked it into her shoulder looked professional.

'Harry?' she said. 'It's me. Give me Joanna.' She waited a moment. 'Joanna?' Her voice relaxed to friendly and conversational. 'Hello, this is Ruth. I'm a friend of Harry and Jane's. I'm a solicitor. Yes. Listen . . . it's getting a bit late for bed and breakfast and anyway I don't suppose you've got much money on you . . . right . . .' She nodded understandingly. 'Well look, how about if we found you a hostel place? Just for tonight . . .' She broke off, listening. Her brow furrowed. 'Well yes, maybe a refuge . . .' She put a hand over the mouthpiece and whispered at me, 'Has she been in a refuge before?'

I thought quickly, and whispered back, 'Yes. Once in Norwich. But I don't think she liked it much.'

Ruth murmured, 'Who does?' then removed her hand from the mouthpiece. Joanna's voice was still speaking. She nodded sympathetically. 'Yes, I know,' she said. 'But they're honestly the best people. You don't want to be on your own tonight. If you don't like it you can leave any time.' She paused, frowning, her head crooked to one side. For a moment there was silence the other end too. Then short, resigned words. Ruth smiled, first into the mouthpiece, and then sideways, at me. 'Right,' she said warmly. 'Leave it with me. It'll be fine, really it will. You go and have a drink with Harry. Tell him to ring back in an hour. We'll have you fixed up by then.'

She put the receiver down. 'Wow,' she said, and exhaled deeply.

I sagged against her. 'You're brilliant,' I sighed. 'Wonderful . . . God, I'd never have managed . . .'

She pushed me away with a short laugh and scraped her chair back. 'Where's my case?' she said, glancing round. She hurried into the hall and returned with a large leather valise.

'The hard part, you realize,' she said, unlocking it, 'is yet to come.' She rummaged among papers and removed a black address book. 'A place in an hour,' she sighed, flicking through the pages, 'Jesus.'

So began a seemingly endless series of phone calls: to numbers that were constantly engaged; or weren't, but still wouldn't answer; or were connected to answering machines that only took messages or gave other numbers; or would reply but couldn't help because the refuge was full and could only suggest yet more numbers; and then just as we were beginning to despair and the hour had been and gone without Harry getting a chance to ring through, we found somewhere. They were crowded and full but immediately grasped the problem, and said she could stay at least for that night, on a sofa if necessary, and that they would help her organize something more long-term in the morning. It was a refuge, so they wouldn't tell us exactly where it was, but it was arranged that if Harry delivered Joanna to a certain café in Holborn at a certain time, a certain woman would be there to meet them, and would take over from there.

Ruth put the receiver down with a groan of relief, and we sat around waiting for Harry to ring in, drumming on surfaces and praying he hadn't been discouraged by finding the line engaged and would try again before it got too late to make the rendezvous. But it only took a long ten minutes or so, and then Ruth snatched up the phone to give him the details, and our part in the rescue was over.

## Chapter 12

Harry didn't come home for hours. The rendezvous had been arranged for nine and we expected him home before ten, but the minutes ticked past the hour with no sign of him. We remembered our missed suppers, and occupied some of the time by preparing and eating a cheese salad. We also drank a large quantity of Martini and wine, initially to relieve the stress and subsequently to celebrate having retrieved at least something from a difficult situation. By eleven, when at last we heard the rumble of the bike outside, I for one was more than mildly sloshed.

We hurried through to the kitchen, and before Harry was halfway through the back door I was pouring out maudlin apologies: a whole evening, God I'm sorry, driving around London sorting out my friend's problems.

Harry waved it all aside magnanimously, looking if anything exhilarated by the experience. Indeed it was hard not to suspect – slightly shockingly – that he had positively enjoyed playing knight on motorized charger.

'How did it go?' Ruth asked excitedly, bobbing up and down beside me. 'Did you get there in time? Is it all right?' Her face – and my own, probably – was scarlet with heat and alcohol. An observer might have found it hard to believe that we were college lecturer and solicitor.

'Hang on,' said Harry, grinning at us. 'Let me get my things off.'

We retreated slightly and the sense of altered movement made me realize that I had been doing a fair bit of bobbing up and down too. Harry dumped the crash helmets on to the draining board and unzipped his leather jacket. He had to jiggle his shoulders before he had any success in removing it. In retaliation for his smugness it crossed my mind that he had become too full of himself to get it off.

'Any food left?' he enquired, finally slinging the jacket on to a chair. He peered into the almost empty bowl of salad on the kitchen table.

'Oh Jesus, just tell us what happened.' Ruth grabbed the plate of salad we had put to one side for him, and thrust it into his stomach.

'Right,' said Harry, inspecting it.

We followed him impatiently into the sitting room. Ruth topped up our glasses with the last of the Martini.

The handover, he announced when we were settled, had been accomplished with total success.

'Oh great,' sighed Ruth.

'Thank God,' I said, feeling the last vestige of tension melt away.

It took a while to get the full story, as Harry seemed to find interest in a blow-by-blow account of his actions hard to fathom. The bald results, he clearly felt, should have been enough. But we did eventually get it.

They'd made the rendezvous, he said, with several minutes to spare.

'In fact the woman was late. Bit put out to see me there, too.'

'Why?' asked Ruth. 'I told them you'd be bringing her.'

Harry shrugged. 'Nobody told her. Quite tetchy about it. Made a point of saying she couldn't tell me where they were taking Joanna. I said fine, I hadn't asked.' He looked amused.

'What about all Joanna's stuff at the bedsit?' I said.

'They'll deal with it tomorrow, when they've helped her sort out a new place. Don't know much more. The woman told me to go then, so they could get back to the refuge.' Harry grinned. 'Nearly choked on my coffee. Asked what the hell she thought I was doing there anyway.'

'Harry,' said Ruth.

'What did she say?' I asked.

'Said she'd been in the job two years and given up wondering what men were doing at all. And would I please just go.'

He shook his head admiringly. It was lucky, I thought, that he was thick-skinned enough to find all this amusing. Chris would have been furious.

'I didn't argue,' Harry went on. 'She looked knackered anyway. Oh, and Joanna says thanks, but then mumbled something about the fewer people who knew the better. I think that means she's not going to be in touch.'

Neither Ruth nor I queried this. In view of my failure to keep one address secret, a reluctance on Joanna's part to trust us with another seemed understandable.

'So where have you been since then?' asked Ruth. 'This must have been hours ago.'

'Went back to Archway,' Harry said.

'What on earth for?'

Harry shrugged. 'Thought I might run into Maskin.'

'And did you?' Ruth's eyes were wide.

'Nope.' He looked regretful. I couldn't help thinking that an encounter would have completed his satisfaction with the evening. He could have challenged Maskin to a trial by combat, to settle the matter once and for all. Not that it would have, of course, but I could almost see Joanna's handkerchief, or whatever latter-day damsels might use to adorn their favourites, blowing from the handlebars of the motorbike. I'm afraid that the mood of relief, with Joanna's whereabouts a mystery even to us, so we were off the hook so to speak, was inspiring in me a kind of hysterical elation, profoundly abetted by the drink.

'But he had been round,' Harry said. 'I knocked up a couple in the bedsit next door and they said someone had called. They told me to ask the landlady, because she always checked visitors out.'

'She does,' I said, nodding wisely.

'Yeah, well, she was a bit shirty at first, it was way past ten. But interested too, you know. She knew it was me Joanna had left with. Maskin had turned up soon afterwards. Must have been him. Polite gent in a suit, she said. He asked for Joanna, and she told him he'd just missed her, she'd gone out with a bloke on a motorbike. She told him to come back tomorrow evening round seven, he'd be bound to catch her in. I said ta very much, I'd be off now.' Harry grinned. 'She turned a bit short again then, started asking questions, wanted to know what Joanna was up to. Nosy cow. Said we owed her an explanation. That's me and Maskin – he asked about me too. I said she'd have to sort it out with Joanna, and left. Then I toured the streets a while, in case Maskin was still hanging around, but no luck.'

Ruth, who had been twisting a curl of hair unhappily round her fingers through this last part, asked, 'Does Maskin know you've got a motorbike?'

This jolted me a little, though it didn't seem to worry Harry. But in any case we decided the answer had to be no, since the bike was kept round the back, and he'd never seen Harry in leathers, or been into their flat, where he might have seen helmets and suchlike.

All the same, it was becoming increasingly clear that if

Maskin had any brain cells at all – and after his performance with the address book we had to credit him with quite a few – he would be bound to assume that if it wasn't actually one of us (i.e. Harry) on the bike, then it had to be someone we knew and had specifically contacted for the operation. He might not assume it tonight, when her absence could be discounted as bad luck, but he would tomorrow, when he discovered she had gone for good.

I found this thought rather sobering (metaphorically only, I'm afraid) and insisted we rethink our positions in the light of it; this didn't get far, though, because Harry wasn't interested – we didn't know anything so we couldn't tell him anything, full stop – and Ruth's and my brain cells had drowned in the torrent of alcohol. Since nothing was likely to have changed by the morning, we elected to sleep on it.

I staggered up the seemingly interminable flights of stairs wrestling with an unco-operatively blank and befuddled mind. But my instincts must still have been operating, because I found myself not only putting the chain on the door, but also locking the mortise from the inside, and bolting the back door below the key, neither of which I usually do when I'm alone in the flat. However, I was too drunk to let these actions unduly alarm me, and recklessly abandoned myself to sleep; and indeed I was still alive and undisturbed in the morning.

The following evening I rang Chris and asked him to come and stay with me. I had seen him at work, but at that stage I was still thinking about what had happened, and Maskin himself, and hadn't exactly established what I felt about it all. But the more I turned it over in my mind the more convinced I became that Maskin had to see us as responsible for Joanna's disappearance, and that he would therefore assume we did now know where she was. And that since he now could have no other routes to her (because any he might have had would be connected to the old place), if he wanted to persist with his quest he would have to come to us. Even if he found out where Joanna worked – perhaps from that garrulous landlady – and tried to get her address from there, it would only be the old one, and if Joanna thought there was the slightest risk of him discovering her actually at work I was sure she'd give it a miss, at least for the time being. So really, that only left us.

I don't think even this would have especially worried me, if I'd been able to believe that Maskin was reasonable and rational in his dealings outside Joanna. I'd simply have expected him to give up. We'd hardly write down a new address for him to repeat yesterday's performance, and he knew we weren't going to part with it voluntarily.

Unfortunately, however, I no longer believed he was either rational or reasonable. It wasn't any one thing, more a combination of smaller things, though overshadowed, inescapably, by the big and sinister question of why, after nearly two years' separation and a divorce, he should still be pursuing someone he must know was terrified of him. But even the smaller things added up. There was his bristling hostility when he first met Harry, an indication – assuming we were right, and he had momentarily viewed him as a boyfriend – that he was prepared to extend aggression to a rival; there was his meek and humble manner otherwise, which alongside his convincing act after seeing the address book I now regarded as worryingly creepy; and there was his ability to ignore the words and actions of others, as if he was so wrapped up in his obsession that nothing else existed for him.

And there was his suit. This may have been overfanciful of me, but I couldn't help finding something deeply disturbing about a man who dressed as if oblivious to the world outside, so that he could still wear a tie and jacket of a fairly heavy material when the temperature was in the eighties, and the rest of us were in shirtsleeves and summer dresses. It suggested to me a mental state held together by clothes, a protective veneer adopted to cling to an illusion of rationality. Because when it came down to it, however much he might plead and complain in seemingly reasonable language, and however superficially well mannered he might appear, what he was doing was not reasonable, or well mannered, and was really exceptionally nasty.

Men like him, Ruth had said, were capable of separating their public and private lives; but what happened, I wondered, when their private lives were stolen from them? It seemed to me that he would be left with a lot of aggression that suddenly found it had nowhere to go; except, perhaps, towards us. Ruth and Harry were all right; he didn't know Ruth from Eve, and she had Harry, and Harry could look after himself. But he knew me, and I was on my own, and possibly couldn't.

But what actually pushed me into action – I'd have rung Chris anyway, but this made it immediate – was a telephone conversation I had with Brian. I meant to speak to Berry, to keep her up to date with events, but I rang too early and she was still out swimming with the children. So I gave it to Brian, only as a kindness to him I softpedalled on the connection Maskin might make between whoever removed Joanna and us (although he could doubtless work it out for himself). I said that while Maskin had discovered that Joanna had left with someone on a motorbike, he had no way of knowing definitely who that person was, and with any luck he'd accept that the trail had petered out.

'Oh good,' Brian said, and then there was a long silence; for a moment I thought we'd been cut off, but we hadn't, and finally he groaned and said he'd remembered something, something about the afternoon Maskin had turned up. Jamie and Zoe had been racing around the garden on their bikes throughout the interview – one of the distracting reasons he'd been less careful than he might have been – and when Jamie heard him give Maskin my name he had started to make roaring motorbike noises and had told Maskin that Aunt Jane lived above a man who had a motorbike and he'd had a ride on it when they came up, and when he was grown up he was going to have one too and wear a black helmet just like Harry.

Brian wasn't sure that Maskin heard all this, because lots of people don't listen to the ramblings of children when they're trying to converse with adults, but it was just possible he had.

This really brought it home to me; the moment I put the phone down I picked it up again to ring Chris, and he said, 'Fine, I'm on my way.'

While I was waiting for him I ran down to tell Harry what Brian had said, since it seemed to point the finger at him as much as me; but he merely shrugged and said, 'So what? He's going to put it down to us anyway, isn't he?'

I had to agree, but I couldn't be as phlegmatic about it as he was.

When Chris arrived he tried to persuade me – gently, but with the unspoken pressure of turning up luggageless – to come back to his house, so I would be right out of any firing line.

I thought about it seriously, but in the end decided I neither wanted nor would be wise to leave now. If Maskin was determined to see me, he would only have to wait – which after all this time he might be rather good at – since I certainly wasn't staying at Chris's indefinitely; and if he got fed up with waiting and chose to take it out on my possessions instead he would have an empty flat to vent his fury on, and I couldn't face the idea of another invasion, possibly more malicious than the last. Also I wanted to be near Ruth and Harry, because

Harry had met Maskin and was, I felt, the only other person who truly understood the situation; and Ruth had the experience and know-how to draw on if the need arose.

I tried to explain all this to Chris without sounding melodramatic or disloyal, and he put his arm round me and murmured, 'It's entirely up to you,' very soothingly.

I was surprised and touched by his tone, and started to wonder if I was appearing more agitated on the surface than I was allowing myself to acknowledge inside. If so, it was an interesting reversal of how I would have expected myself to react.

I pondered this as we drove back to his house to pick up everything he needed for a fortnight – an arbitrary period, just to establish the arrangement as temporary – and forgot it in the physical effort of lugging the boxes and bundles home to the flat. It all looked cosily domestic when his work books and clothes were mixed in with mine, flannels and toothbrushes nestling together in the bathroom; and, as I regarded the connubial scene with very churned-up emotions, Chris stretched himself out comfortably on the sitting room sofa and tried to hide the satisfied gleam in his eye.

## Chapter 13

Nothing much happened for the first week. I say nothing much, but I mean to us. Lots seemed to be happening in the world outside, and because Chris was actually living with me we tended to stay in more, indulging in those domestic pursuits that homely couples get up to, such as watching television and reading the newspapers, so I was even more aware of events than usual. Or maybe it was simply my state of mind and what caught my eye; I daresay any week can provide evidence to suggest the human race is beyond redemption. Singhalese mobsters were slaughtering Tamils in Sri Lanka, literally stopping buses on the roads, taking all the Tamil men off and butchering them; Hindus were battling with Sikhs in unfamiliar parts of India, and it wasn't clear who was avenging themselves on whom for what; a police station in Northern Ireland was mortared by the IRA, killing two policemen and three teenage passers-by; and the papers were full of mind-numbing details of a trial involving a hooded maniac who got his kicks from terrorizing young couples in their cars, forcing them to do unspeakable things to each other, and then raping the woman and torturing the man. He hadn't actually killed anyone, but this was more by luck than judgement.

Thankfully this case merited no more than a few subdued inches on the front page of the *Guardian*, with the full report tucked away inside, and not much on the television, because there weren't many pictures to go with it. Just a few shots of the various leafy lanes where the horrors had occurred, and a report from Our Correspondent in Court, overlooked by a murky artist's impression of the hooded monster himself, as he would have appeared to his victims, staring out from behind the correspondent's left ear. But of course it was front page RAPE TORTURE HORROR in all the tabloids, which I couldn't help but notice as inconsiderate people left them lying around the staff room at work, and doubtless all the revolting if irresistible details were spelt out with glee and prurience inside. Which of the staff bought these papers was a mystery – possibly they remained anonymous for fear of censure from the rest of us – but I told Chris if I had my way I'd make their purchase an immediate disqualification from the job of inculcating in young people minimum standards of honesty and decent behaviour, which is what we were always being told teaching was coincidentally about.

And we saw some minor mayhem of our own, when we visited a couple of pubs on Kilburn High Road. (Not one of our usual haunts, but there didn't seem much point in using the car when we were starting and finishing at the same place.)

Some of the pubs on the High Road had a reputation for trouble; not of a particularly vicious kind, more the Saturday-night-brawl, or hopelessly inebriated kind. The residents of Kilburn are a cosmopolitan lot: as well as the English we had a good number of Asians (rarely seen in pubs, perhaps because they were Muslim, or too busy manning their late-night shops) but we also had the Irish, the menfolk of whom were invariably found in pubs, or propped up outside them with an empty glass from the morning session, waiting for the doors to reopen, and who seemed fond of a little rough and tumble to end off a glorious drinking day.

Despite this (and unrelated to the fact that two of my own great-grandfathers were Dubliners) I have a sneaking affection for the Irish. Their line in patter – when you can decipher it – is entrancing, they never seem to attack anyone except their best friends, and they are unfailingly polite to outsiders even mid-brawl. At least that has been my experience. Once, with a group of friends, as we hesitated outside a High Road pub, the women waiting for the men to lead the way in, a man grasping a broken bottle came hurtling towards us from another entrance; he slowed as he saw us and then politely ushered us aside with lilting apologies of 'Excuse me, ladies and gents,' before plunging through the double doors to join the mêlée. Before the doors swung to again we had a tantalizing – almost surreal – glimpse of a vast man with a monumental pot belly holding a chair aloft, presumably to bring crashing down on someone's head. We all looked at each other as if to confirm that what we had seen was not a hallucination, and then unanimously decided to try another pub.

However, Chris and I saw nothing as memorable during our week. We stuck to the saloons and snugs and heard occasional jostlings from the public bars, and outside saw a few men recovering in the gutter from action within, but none of this was as intimidating as, say, a late-night tube trip from Leicester Square could be, even if you never saw any violence. Just a glimpse of all those dangerous-looking inebriates and junkies was enough to make me dig in my purse for the taxi fare. Irish drunks on their own stamping ground didn't give off nearly such menacing vibrations.

And domestic life with Chris was really quite bearable. There was twice as much washing to do, but that was dropped off as usual at the launderette down the road (the manageress did it for me and folded everything so professionally I virtually never had to iron). I suppose I put a little more thought into food, although we went out once to the vegetarian Vijay nearby, a restaurant heavily patronized by local Indians, proving it authentic, or so I optimistically imagined. And Chris was not an untidy person. Indeed, he was noticeably tidier than I was, so perhaps it was as well we were at my place and not his. Three years on your own and having to cope singlehanded with visiting daughters would probably be enough to housetrain anyone, though in fact I think he'd always been fairly competent on the home front. A natural domestic orderliness – lapsing occasionally into fussiness – seemed very much in character.

I did all the shopping during the week but he did more than his fair share of cooking, and whilst he was a bit apt to follow instructions, and worried if he hadn't got exactly the right quantities of this and that, as if a recipe was a chemical formula that might result in explosion or a different meal altogether if not followed to the nearest tenth of an ounce, all his contributions were successes. Lasagne and Quiche Lorraine tasted much nicer to me than they usually did, mostly because I hadn't cooked them.

Really the only drawback of his being there – excluding lack of time to myself, which for once wasn't an issue – was having to let him drive me to and from college every day. His insurance didn't cover me, and anyway it would have been the height of rudeness to make him hand over the keys for the duration. However, if the traffic was reasonable the journey only took twenty minutes, so I tried to look on it as a small price to pay (God willing) for his company and protection, and made an effort to keep my mouth shut.

As far as his guard duties were concerned – the *raison d'être* of the arrangement, after all – the routine was that he would open the door to callers, and answer the telephone. This latter duty was added after I had a couple of those disconcerting calls where you say 'Hello?' and nobody answers, though you're sure someone is listening at the other end. I'd had similar calls – and worse – before, and normally they made me cross, rather than frightening me. If they were actually whispering something naughty I'd keep repeating briskly, 'I'm sorry, the line's very bad, you'll have to speak up,' and if they fell for it bang the phone down mid-bellow. Or just occasionally, with persistent offenders, put on a little-girl voice and lisp, 'Stinky bottom ha ha ha,' at them before disconnecting the phone. Trading crudities with perverts is probably not recommended, but it made me feel better.

However, this week it was different, because of Maskin, and because having a face to put to the caller made it seem more worrying, not less so. The calls stopped when Chris started answering them, which proved nothing, of course, but gave the stress muscles in my throat a rest, and made him feel useful.

My rules for his door-opening duty were straightforward and specific: he was only to open the door on the chain, and if it were Maskin he was to close it again immediately, toes, feet, hands notwithstanding. He wasn't to believe a word Maskin said, however reasonably he said it, and on no account was he to be tempted into face-to-face confrontation, whatever the provocation. He was to stay with me on our side of the door, and if necessary we would summon help by phone. And that was that, no deviations permitted.

It felt odd preparing like this for events that might exist only in my imagination, but on the other hand there seemed little point in having Chris there without a plan in case those events were realized. And if Chris was being put, albeit willingly, into the role of my protector, then the least I could do was lay ground rules that not only minimized the risk to both of us but excluded any kind of discretionary action on his part. It might not give him the chance to be heroic, but neither would it give him the chance to feel bad about being unheroic; this seemed, with memories of past confrontations to mind, a most desirable compromise.

I told Chris the rules without going deeply into motives, except for stressing that I wanted him with me, and wanted me the other side of a closed door from Maskin, a sentiment I thought sounded convincingly female enough.

But evidently it wasn't; he looked at me and after a pause nodded, gave me a lopsided smile and said, 'Right, I'll cancel the bull-worker then.' And luckily I laughed so much it quite covered my embarrassment at being seen through so easily.

It wasn't until the Saturday at the end of the first week that we had a break in routine. We went to a wedding. Chris's cousin Madeline, a botanist at Kew Gardens, was doing her bit for endangered species by marrying her local curate. I'm not normally a fan of weddings – too many coy 'Your turn next?' nudges when I was younger – but I found myself anticipating this one like a holiday. It was to be a wholehog white wedding at a Richmond church, and a marquee reception on someone's lawn afterwards.

I selected my most Jane Austen-like dress to wear – a demure beige silk number – and for once thoroughly enjoyed the titivating process. Nails, teeth, make-up, hair – which I wore up, having drawn the line at a hat.

Settling into the taxi for the outward journey (Chris wanted to be able to drink) I felt positively frivolous. The flats, Maskin and domesticity were behind us; champagne and the quaint mating rituals of the semi-urbanized county classes beckoned.

'I didn't think anyone married curates these days,' I said to Chris light-headedly. 'I thought they were all gay.'

Chris frowned, fiddling with the knot of his paisley tie.
'Robert plays rugger,' he muttered.

I laughed and kissed him on the nose.

He glanced at me with a half-smile. 'What's with you? I
thought you hated weddings.'

'I do.' I sat back complacently. 'Especially white ones.
Virgins were decked out in white for dragons, you know.'

Chris pulled a sour face. 'Well, sounds appropriate then,
doesn't it?'

I grinned. I was aware that today was likely to be an ordeal,
not a treat, for Chris. However, he hadn't admitted this, so I
was disregarding it too.

'What's she like, cousin Madeline?' I asked. I'd never met
bride or groom.

Chris shrugged. 'Haven't seen her for years. Brainy. She's a
specialist in succulents.'

I curled over on the seat. 'A succulent specialist . . . oh,
wonderful. But is she?'

'Is she what?'

'Succulent.'

Chris laughed, despite himself. 'Wait and see.'

The church was small and exquisitely spired – just the sort of
place that, as a tourist, I'd have happily popped into to kill an
hour. A star-shaped stained-glass window dappled the guests
and dark wood pews with colour as romantic as candlelight.
The only faces I recognized were those of Chris's parents, a tall
wispy couple in their late fifties who smiled bravely at us as we
passed to our seats. They had seen the marriages of both their
own children end in acrimonious divorce.

I wouldn't have described Madeline as succulent; but who
can look remotely juicy encased in yards of stiff white tulle and
taffeta? Walking down the aisle on her father's arm she looked
to me much like any other church-wedding bride – pale and

icon-like and charmingly terrified. The groom, Robert, was a heavily built young man with a receding hairline and honest, golden retriever eyes. He was perspiring heavily in his pale grey suit and, unlike Madeline, looked solidly flesh and blood. I suppose it's an intentional visual paradox that at the moment of ritual union man and woman should appear so disparate.

My light-headed frame of mind survived the service and was only temporarily dimmed by an overlong photographic session in the churchyard. It lifted again as soon as I was in the marquee, with a glass of champagne in my hand.

All this effort, I thought benignly, tucked in at Chris's elbow as we cruised the sea of introductions to friends and relatives. All this expense and goodwill. How could anyone have so many uncles? What a lot of white handbags.

At some point I became detached from Chris and spent half an hour chatting to an elderly gentleman propped on silver-topped canes who told me – and I decided to take it as a compliment – that I reminded him of his mother. It must have been the dress. Before I could decide whether he was rich and frail enough to be worth pursuing he was hustled away by a busy matron, who was possibly his daughter, to take his 'medication'. Then I joined a female conversation on teenage daughters: mothers talking with a mixture of agony and pride of their offsprings, two of whom were stomping round the garden in the surreal combination of lilac satin bridesmaid's dresses and Nike trainers.

'Thank goodness,' said one mother in heartfelt tones, 'that Sammy's first love is still her pony.'

*Oh yes*, I thought, mentally hugging myself, and nodded emphatic support.

I eventually rejoined Chris inside the marquee, by the vol-au-vent table.

'Marry me,' I whispered, snuggling up to him. He looked delicious: very blond and young and wearing his hunted expression, as he always did within Dear Boy range of his parents. I gestured at the throng. 'Only you can give me all this.'

'You're drunk,' he said, visibly relaxing, and slipped his arm around my waist.

I leant against him. 'Only a little. I don't want to go home. I want to live in fairyland for ever.'

'Cynic.'

'Realist,' I said. 'I expect Joanna and Maskin got married in church.'

'Come on. Robert's a curate. They'll be OK.'

'Maybe,' I said. I rested my head against Chris's shoulder. A few yards away a smart young woman in an orange suit was leaning over the buffet table, unfurling rolls of Parma ham with a fork and carefully picking out the asparagus.

'Cheek,' I murmured. Chris didn't reply. I looked up at his face. He was staring at a point on the far side of the marquee.

'D'you mind this?' I asked softly. Chris and Alyssia had been married at a registry office. But marriage is marriage, wherever.

He glanced at me, then back at the distance. After a moment he said, 'Of course not.'

I found his hand and squeezed it. Liar, I thought.

We left at four, soon after the speeches. Chris said he had a headache from the champagne, but I think he was just feeling overwhelmed. I didn't mind; all good things have to end.

When we got back to the flat Chris lay down on the sofa and accepted a cup of tea and two paracetamol. I slipped off my silk dress and took a shower. And then, because I was thinking about Chris, lying there feeling sorry for himself in his suit, while I was wet and refreshed and naked, I put my contraceptive cap in. Wrapped in a towel I went into the sitting room and sat on the side of the sofa. Chris grumbled that my hair was dripping on him, but his hands were already at my breasts, and once the towel had fallen away he stopped complaining.

We played around a while before I let him get undressed. I know it was the circumstances, more than any special chemistry between us, that made me enjoy the session so much; but who cares? We were a couple, and couples create excitement where they can.

# Chapter 14

On the Wednesday of the second week Maskin appeared again. And I was right to have been fearful, because it was frightening, although he didn't step a foot into the flat, and nobody got hurt, unless you count damaged nerve-endings.

Chris and I had just got back from college. It was too early for Ruth to be home, and there had been silence downstairs when we passed their front door, which meant Harry was out too. He wasn't working at the time; summer is the motorcyclist's season and he needed to be free to take off when the mood struck.

It was stiflingly hot again, especially in my flat, being right under the roof, and all the flies and moths in the neighbourhood had congregated in the hall to greet us. Just as we were walking round opening windows, bemoaning the stuffiness, a tapping began on the front door.

This was odd; I had a perfectly functioning bell, and only someone who was blind, or very distracted, could have failed to notice it. The tapping was curious too: continuous, with no gaps for a response, as if the caller was hooked on the action, or was tapping out some message in code to conspirators within.

I stood in the kitchen doorway and stared at the front door. It has to be kids, I thought. There was a short curtain hanging over the frosted glass so no one could see the movements of people inside, but it also meant that I couldn't see shapes of visitors outside either. Nobody is very recognizable through frosted glass, but distinguishing between an adult and a child should be possible, I thought, unless – ridiculous notion – the adult was crouching.

Chris emerged from the sitting room. He gave me a puzzled frown, and walked to the front door. I opened my mouth to say, 'Look through the glass first,' but he was already turning the latch.

Of course Chris had never met Maskin. But I had given him a description; and in doing so ended up with a picture much more potentially harmful than I'd started with. Because of his manner I'd seen him as smaller than he really was. But Harry, whose help I enlisted, said he was at least as tall as he was, and it's something one's usually aware of, your own height *vis-à-vis* someone else's. And he wasn't a slightly built man either, considered objectively, though the way he held himself gave you that impression.

Chris took a quick look and immediately closed the door again. 'I think it's him,' he said quietly.

The tapping had stopped. I walked over and to check, thinking I'd probably recognize him even all fuzzy behind the glass, flicked the curtain back. A squashed, pale shape – a face, I suddenly realized, grotesquely distorted – was pressed up against it.

'Christ!' I gasped, leaping back about ten foot and leaving most of my wits behind. 'Jesus Christ!'

Chris looked alarmed, then angry. 'Is that you, Maskin?' He confronted the closed door. 'What the hell are you playing at?'

'Miss Hardy?' Maskin's voice drifted in to us. 'Miss Hardy, are you there?'

'Go away,' I said.

'Please, Miss Hardy.' The voice took on a whiny, singsong quality. 'I just want to know how she is. Let me in, please. Just for a few minutes.'

'No,' I said.

'You're her friend, I only want to talk to you. I won't look for her, I promise. It's not much to ask. Just a few minutes of your time. Let me in. Miss Hardy, please.'

I found his tone terrifying; I didn't believe him, and, even more frightening, was suddenly convinced he didn't intend me to. It was in the whine, a horrid knowing edge that seemed to be saying: see, I'll say nothing you can complain about, nothing you can hold against me, but I can frighten you all the same, and there's nothing you can do about it.

I shook my head violently at Chris, panicked by the thought that he might not have heard the same, and might be going to open the door. But it was all right: he'd heard at least a hint, and looked appalled. Which should have been a relief, but wasn't.

'Miss Hardy doesn't want to discuss anything with you,' he said tightly. 'Go away.'

'Miss Hardy?' Maskin whined. 'Please, Miss Hardy?'

'Go away,' I whispered.

Maskin did know what he was doing, and was trying to intimidate rather than genuinely persuade us, or he wouldn't have done what he did next. For a moment there was quiet, then the brass letter box flap below the curtain opened, and he began to rhythmically snap it up and down.

The flesh on my back crawled. The slot was only letter-sized – at most nine inches by three – but in my mind's eye I could see Maskin oozing through, and I knew he was doing it to frighten me.

'I can't take this,' I whispered to Chris, and fled into the sitting room. Through the pounding of blood in my ears I heard Chris's voice, hard with anger, saying, 'If you don't leave this instant I'm going to ring the police.'

Maskin's voice started to reply. I covered my ears, reducing the sound to a distant floating wail. It went on so long I began to wonder if it was still Maskin, or whether I had picked up some animal cry outside. Or if I was making the noise myself, in my head. Then I heard Chris's voice over it, raised to me. I removed my hands.

'I'm going to ring the police now,' he called. 'OK?'

'Yes, please.' The act of speech made me aware that I was standing, revolving slowly, in the centre of the room. I stopped, found myself facing the sofa, and sat down on it.

I heard the sound of Chris flicking through the phone book. I nodded to myself, guessing he was looking for the number of the local police station; that's right, I thought, they know about Maskin.

Then I realized that that was all I could hear. The wailing had stopped.

'Is he still there?' I called softly.

For a moment there was silence. I imagined Chris's head turned to the door, listening.

'Yes,' he murmured.

Perhaps Maskin didn't think we'd actually do it, because it wasn't until Chris got through to the police, and I had crept back to the hall to join him, that there was a shuffle of movement outside the door. We heard the creak of linoleum and boards on the landing, and then the slow receding plod of feet descending the stairs.

While Chris was still talking I regathered my wits – more accessible now the spectre had retreated – and went to the study window to check he was really going. I saw him as he appeared on the path below, almost human again now that he was fully visible, and still wearing that horrible suit.

Just as he reached the gap in the low garden wall where the path meets the road, there was a roar of engine noise.

I looked left. A large black motorbike was detaching itself from the rush hour traffic. It crossed the carriageway, bounced up the kerb on to the pavement and came thundering towards Maskin.

'Christ!' I shrieked. Harry was going to mow him down, there and then.

Maskin clearly thought the same; he shot back behind the wall, cast around wildly, and then started to run towards the other gap, in front of the main doors.

But Harry wouldn't let him escape that way either. He swung the bike round, arm-flagging the traffic to a standstill as he crashed down the kerb and up again, and roared back towards him.

Within an arm's length of the gap Maskin lost his nerve, and swerved aside. Harry cut the escape off, and, feet from the desperately flailing, backtracking figure, gunned the engine with the clutch in. The noise must have been deafening outside: I found it terrorizing, even from two storeys up and with the glass between us.

Chris arrived beside me. 'What the hell?' he cried, above the noise, and then taking in the scene below breathed, 'Jee-sus.'

Maskin stumbled away from the bike and began to run back towards our entrance. Panic had set in: arms pumped empty air, legs danced and skittered; twice he slipped on the scrubby grass, twisting to see over his shoulder.

Harry turned the bike again, standing up on the footrests to bump down the kerb. A Mini driver had to pull sharply wide to avoid him, and stalled in the middle of the road. Up on the pavement again Harry stopped the bike and waited, legs braced against the ground. The machine pulled against him ominously, as if it were alive, and only just restrained.

Maskin took two hesitant sideways steps on to the pavement, saw Harry's feet lift, and as the bike roared towards him flung himself back behind the wall. Staggering clumsily up on to the grass he tripped, failed to recover his balance, and sat down heavily.

Harry braked at the gap, threw up his helmet visor and shouted something. I doubted Maskin could grasp the words over the engine noise, but it certainly added to the overall nerve-shredding impact, which was probably what Harry was after.

Chris hissed, 'Bloody idiot!' in my ear. It took a moment for his words to register. I was seeing the bike in relation to the gap; if he'd wanted to, Harry could have taken it through. But he hadn't. That first charge had looked so convincing.

Maskin scrambled to his feet and set off across the grass again. He slipped and slid around with such loss of dignity that I could scarcely bear to watch. I wanted to shout to him to stop, and brazen it out; although I feared and hated the man I felt for him too, made to look so ridiculous and pathetic. My feelings towards Harry defied expression; I was paralysed between the urgent desire to hurtle downstairs and tell him to stop it, at once, this minute, and the overwhelming temptation to bury my head in my hands and pretend the whole exhibition had nothing whatsoever to do with me.

But by now a crowd of passers-by had collected on the opposite pavement. The traffic had ground to a standstill too, partly out of interest, and partly because Harry was using so much of the road for his turns. Two shirt-sleeved young men were actually out of their cars, shouting what could have been a commentary to each other across the vehicles.

Maskin at last seemed to realize that if Harry had been intending to damage him he would have done it by now and not waited until half the street was gathered to witness it.

He let Harry turn the bike again, and then at first nervously, but with growing determination, stepped out from the protection of the wall. As Harry roared up and whipped past he faltered, but recovered himself and pressed on.

Harry braked a short distance beyond, turned in the saddle, and yelled something back at him. Maskin lowered his gaze, but kept his pace steady.

Harry allowed him to pass, then let rip with the throttle and edged the bike forwards. He appeared to have settled for escort duty. He rode very slowly abreast of Maskin and judging from the emphatic jerks of his helmet and punctuating throttle bursts, was still haranguing him. Side by side, they disappeared from view.

Haltingly, the traffic began to move again. The pavement crowd turned inward, with a flurry of words and gestures, then loosened itself with more restrained smiles and headshakes, and appeared about to disperse.

Chris said, 'Thank God,' with a groaning sigh, and pushed himself away from the window.

I caught his arm.

'Wait,' I said sinkingly, still gazing out. 'Look.'

The crowd opposite was rebunching. Parts of it, suddenly uncontainable with excitement, began to surge across the road. The slow-moving traffic ground to a halt again. Directly below us, pulling up on to the pavement with hazard lights flashing, was the emblazoned, crime-confirming lines of a police patrol car.

Chris made a distressed noise in his throat. At least a dozen people were flocking round the policecar. Eager arms and fingers pointed down the road.

'They're ours,' I said urgently. 'They must be. We'll have to go down.' I tugged at Chris's sleeve. 'Chris, come on.'

I banged my thigh on the corner of the study table, rushing

for the front door. Then I couldn't get the door open – I think I was wrenching at it too hard to get the chain off – and with a cry of frustration had to stand back to let Chris do it. We crashed down the stairs. Inside my head a succession of wildly constructed explanations soared – we didn't know the biker, he was nothing to do with us – we did, we'd rung him too, he was only trying to catch the man – we didn't know either of them, truly, it was just a massive coincidence – and in the descending jolts, collapsed to mental rubble.

Just inside the double doors I made Chris stop, for a silent, brain-restoring moment. Then we stepped outside.

I'd forgotten how hot and bright the day was. It was like stepping out under arc lights. Ahead of us the police officers stood backed against the patrol car, barely visible behind the crowd.

As we approached, voices in the babble became distinct. 'Bloody maniac!' I heard, and 'Stopped all the traffic!' and urgently, 'You'd get him, if you went now!'

I found myself shouldering a path, with an aggressiveness that astonished me, to the front line.

'Hello,' I said loudly. 'Thanks for coming so quickly.'

The policemen's heads swung round. They were both hatless and in shirtsleeves. I said, 'Oh, hello,' again. The officer nearest me was the blond young constable Ruth and I had spoken to a fortnight ago. Having prepared myself for inventions, I couldn't decide if this was a good or bad thing.

'Nearly killed him, he did!' a fat scarlet-faced man in the crowd said indignantly. 'Bloody great bike, could have killed him, easy.' He nodded round for group confirmation. A chorus of voices agreed.

'The man we called you about has just gone,' I said, loudly again. 'A neighbour frightened him away.'

The other officer, dark and bearded to high on the

cheekbones, was frowning at the scarlet-faced man. Slowly his gaze returned to me. The frown deepened.

'We called you,' I insisted. 'At least my boyfriend did.' I'd lost Chris. I swivelled blindly, and found him just behind me. Breathlessly I said, 'He called you.'

Chris stepped forward. I pressed a trembling hand to my breast bone. The violence of my reactions was frightening me.

'You called us, sir, did you?' the bearded officer asked.

'Er, yes,' said Chris. 'There was a man trying to . . . um . . . force his way into my girlfriend's flat.'

'The man I was telling you about last week,' I said, to the blond constable. My voice came out jerky, but calmer. 'The one looking for his ex-wife. He didn't find her, so he came back. He kept banging on the door, asking to speak to me. He wouldn't go away.'

'I see.' The officer nodded, digesting this. His partner stared blankly at Chris, as if he didn't see at all. Mottled pink patches began to appear on Chris's cheeks. Someone behind me complained, 'He'll be all the way to Timbuctoo by now,' eliciting a grumble of agreement from the crowd.

A distracted ripple passed through the frown of the bearded policeman. 'This would have been,' he said, making a conspicuous effort to concentrate on us, 'while your boyfriend was there?'

'Well, yes,' I said. Chris's pinkness darkened to a deep blush. It took me a moment to grasp why. 'I made him ring you,' I added earnestly. 'I was terrified.'

Before we could receive a response to this there was an eruption of excitement from the crowd.

'There he is!' several voices cried.

'He's coming back!' shouted several more.

I was pushed forward by someone craning for a better

view and had to clutch Chris's arm for support. Scarlet-face –
no, purple-face now – bulldozed a path to the policemen.

'That's him!' he roared, gesticulating furiously down the
road. 'That's him, that's the one!'

I recovered my balance and strained to see over the jostling
shoulders of the crowd. A hundred yards away, cruising
steadily towards us – though mercifully on the carriageway
now, tucked in among the approaching northbound traffic –
was a large black motorbike. In my left ear – Chris's side – I
heard a heartfelt groan.

The policemen began to push through the crowd to open
pavement. I struggled desperately in their wake. 'That's not
the man,' I gasped. 'That's the neighbour who got rid of him.
He was just trying to help.'

We broke through the crowd in front of the patrol car. The
policemen stopped at the kerb and in my eagerness to keep up
with them I almost collided with their backs. The bike
thudded towards us. A few cars' lengths away it moved to the
white line in the centre of the road. A gloveless hand lifted to
us in salute.

The bearded officer shouted, 'Oi!' stepped off the kerb a
foot from the bumper of the policecar, and pointed per-
emptorily at the ground between his feet.

Harry slowed, then at a break in the southbound traffic
swung the bike across the carriageway, and drew up in front of
us.

The air thrummed with engine noise. The policeman
opened his mouth, thought better of it, and made an impatient
chopping movement with his hand. I could see Harry's eyes,
smiling at him, as he reached down to cut the engine. The
throb of the motor was replaced by a thrilled buzz from the
crowd.

Harry sat back on the saddle, loosened his helmet and

removed it, revealing hair and face glistening with sweat. He grinned round at everyone, looking hugely pleased with himself.

'He arrived after I'd rung you,' I said urgently, trying to give Harry – and everybody else who hadn't yet grasped it – the order of events. 'He was only trying to keep the man here.'

'You ought to be ashamed of yourself,' the purple-faced man called, from a safe distance. 'You could have killed him.'

Harry twisted on the saddle to look at him. Cheerfully he called back, 'Yeah, could have done, couldn't I?' He shook his head regretfully, as if it were a bright idea he wished he'd thought of at the time.

Several members of the crowd ticked censoriously at this. Oh God, I thought. Chris, appearing the far side of the young policeman, snapped, 'Stow it, Harry.'

Both officers looked disapproving, but still primarily puzzled. The bearded policeman laid a palm on the handlebars of the bike. 'Off,' he said.

Harry dismounted, alarming the crowd into fluttering retreat, and lifted the bike up on to its stand. With a satisfied, end-of-mission air he unzipped his leather jacket, peeled it off, and tossed it over the petrol tank. His T-shirt was soaked with sweat; he tugged the front out of his jeans and flapped it about in the hot air. The crowd cautiously edged in again, seeming to find him less threatening now the man beneath the leather was revealed.

In careful, tension-defusing tones, the policemen asked for his name, address, age, and an account of what, exactly, he had been doing.

I suppose Harry replied, though in fact I heard little except the stuck-record drone of my own voice, repeating at intervals, 'He's a neighbour, he was only trying to help.' I said it at least a dozen times; it was partly shock, I think, and partly the gabble-inducing conviction that Harry was incapable of saying anything to help himself. It didn't seem to achieve much in the policemen's minds – twice they turned round to tell me I'd made my point, and I made it several times after that – but with the crowd I think it did: it seemed gradually to percolate group consciousness that the persecuted victim had not been an innocent member of the public, but rather a wanted, and possibly dangerous, suspect. The purple-faced man grumbled, 'So what, he still ought to be locked up,' but this time drew only half-hearted mumbles of support. A few individuals at the fringe of the crowd began to wander away.

The policemen stepped back from Harry to include Chris and myself in the conversation. I felt my mouth close with a snap.

'This man Maskin . . .' The young officer spoke slowly, but as if fairly confidently on track. 'Where is he now?'

Chris and I lifted arms to point down the road.

'Halfway to Queen's Park tube,' Harry said.

'How long ago was this?'

'Ten minutes?' said Chris.

'Less,' said Harry.

The officers looked at each other. 'Worth a try,' the young one said. With a thumb he indicated Chris and myself. 'Take one of them.'

The bearded officer nodded and said to Chris, 'Want to ride shotgun?' He began to walk to the car.

Chris started to follow, then hesitated. 'D'you want to go?' he said to me. 'Maybe . . .'

'No,' I said definitely. 'You go.'

I watched them climb into the car. Chris closed the door and sat forward, gazing intently at the dash. As he pulled the seat belt across I saw him say something to the officer, with a sidelong, almost shy, half-smile. Despite everything I nearly smiled too. I guessed it was his first ride in a policecar.

With the disappearance of the car the remains of the crowd drifted away. The scarlet-faced man lingered briefly, more disgruntled now, it seemed, by the inaction of the police and the defections around him, than with Harry. He stared balefully around and then jabbed a finger at the young officer and said warningly, 'You tell him, right?'

The officer ignored him. Harry grinned at me, a grin broadening, as if vastly entertained, when I refused to smile back.

The officer squatted down on the kerb to inspect the bike. Harry transferred the grin to him, then with a sigh of content yanked his T-shirt off over his head and started to dry his armpits with it.

The officer stood up. His expression was non-committal. 'Got documents on you?' he asked.

'Sure,' said Harry. He gave his chest a passing rub with the T-shirt, then dug in the lining of the jacket flung over the petrol tank of the bike and handed him a clear plastic wallet.

We waited while each document was studied carefully. I still didn't trust myself to speak directly to Harry, and he had his damp neck and stomach and inner triumph to occupy him, so nothing was said.

The officer slipped the papers back into the wallet. 'Nice machine,' he said neutrally. 'You do it up yourself?'

'Yup.' Harry took the wallet from him and tucked it back into the jacket.

The policeman nodded to himself. In the same unladen tone he said, 'You're aware, are you, that it's an offence to ride a motorbike on the pavement? You know that, do you?'

'Yup,' said Harry again, smiling.

'He's a very good driver usually,' I said, forcing myself. 'It was only because he recognized Maskin. He knew he'd been bothering me. Normally he's very sensible, honestly.'

'Is he,' said the officer.

Harry gave me a look of deep amusement. 'Very sensible,' he agreed. As if the matter was of minor importance, and now settled, he dropped to his heels and started to dab at dust streaks on the chrome exhaust of the bike with the scrunched-up T-shirt.

The policeman looked down at him, chewing something indigestible at the corner of his mouth. In a moment of fury – for being forced to defend someone who refused to defend himself, and whose actions had been indefensible anyway – I contemplated leaving a vicious red handmark on the smooth expanse of Harry's back.

Just then the patrol car reappeared, from the right, among the southbound traffic. I saw the car before I could see the occupants, and found myself retreating from the kerb. Harry got to his feet as it passed, obscuring my view. The car mounted the pavement beyond, in front of the main entrance to the flats. My backward progress was only halted by my heel grazing the concrete of the low garden wall. Though the rear seat of the car, I was almost sure, had been empty.

Chris got out. The casual force with which he slammed the car door suggested that policecars had become a routinely unimpressive form of transport. He glanced at the two by the bike and then walked over to me, shaking his head.

'No sign of him. He must have reached the tube station.' He sounded undisappointed. The relaxing of something inside me told me I was too. He dropped his voice. 'I don't know what they'd have done with him anyway. Probably just as well.'

The young officer had joined his partner by the patrol car. They conferred. A beckoning hand waved Harry over.

'What's happening?' Chris asked softly. 'Are they going to book him?'

I looked at the group. It was two against one now – worrying, on the face of it – but it had been earlier, and in front of spectators then, too. There were no notebooks or radios in use. 'I'm not sure,' I said. 'Maybe not. If he behaves himself. He might just get a ticking off.'

'Looks like we're all in danger of that,' Chris murmured. He tipped his head toward the flats. 'By the main door.'

I followed his gaze. Framed in the open doorway of the main entrance was the tiny figure of Mrs Rosen. She was wearing a sleeveless dress of astonishing garishness – acid green, splashed with screaming sunflowers – reminiscent of her sitting room carpet. Even at this distance I could detect the eager quiver of flesh. Most of the action, I realized, had taken place just outside her net curtains.

I was about to make a sour aside to Chris when my eye was caught by another figure, equally familiar, on the pavement a hundred and fifty yards beyond the policecar. Dressed in brown and cream, hair coppery in the sunlight, hurrying towards us.

'It's Ruth!' I hissed. 'Oh God.' My insides clamped into a knot. The thought of what she was seeing, and must be imagining, was excruciating. I looked back at the group by the car, and wished fervently, though obscurely, that Harry had kept more of his clothes on. Through gritted teeth I whispered, 'Grovel, you stupid man, grovel.'

But in fact watching them now, my anxiety eased. Harry was standing with his back to us, an arm crooked at his side, thumb tucked into the front pocket of his jeans: an attitude if not of meekness at least of negligent good grace. In front of him the fair officer leant against the policecar, shirtsleeved elbow resting on the roof. He was talking with some animation, turning first to his partner, then Harry. The bearded officer stood with arms folded across his chest, one hand raised, stroking his beard. As I watched the hand was removed and he said something, gesturing with a twisting motion at the bike. Harry glanced back at it, shook his head, and grasping an invisible object in front of him rotated it sharply. The heads of both officers tilted back, their mouths opening in 'Ah's of comprehension. I almost copied them; what I was watching, I suddenly realized, was no longer any kind of confrontation, but a meeting of mechanical male minds.

Ruth's approach broke the group up. Harry lifted a relaxed, welcoming arm to her, and the officers, as if recollecting themselves, and reluctant to become embroiled in third-party explanations, turned for the car. The bearded officer called a cursory, 'Off the pavement, mind!' as he walked round to the driver's door.

Harry made no acknowledgement; he hadn't waited for Ruth to reach him but was strolling back towards the bike. Ruth's pace lost urgency; the anxiety in her face, as her gaze moved from the departing policecar to Harry, was replaced by grim enquiry.

Harry picked up his clothes and helmet from the bike, waited for her to reach him, and dumped them in her arms. He grinned at her. 'Cheer up,' he said. 'It might never happen.' He added a jaunty wave over her shoulder to the distant Mrs Rosen.

Ruth swung round in confusion and almost lost her grip on the helmet. Harry laughed lightly at her, pushed the motorbike off its stand, and started to wheel it away.

I walked quickly over to Ruth. I couldn't think what sense of nicety – stupidly misplaced – had stopped me intervening earlier.

'It's all right,' I said reassuringly. 'We had some trouble but it's OK now.'

She was frowning after Harry. 'What trouble?' she said. She turned her gaze to me. 'For God's sake,' she said frustratedly, 'what's OK now?'

A glimpse of acid-green movement made me hesitate. Mrs Rosen, perhaps encouraged by Harry's wave, was trotting down the path. Without blatant rudeness retreat would soon be impossible.

I grasped Ruth's arm. 'Inside,' I said, pulling her towards our entrance. 'I'll tell you inside.'

In fact Chris explained. I was too exhausted. It hit me, violently and disablingly, and mostly in the legs, the moment we were inside their flat. I staggered through to the sitting room sofa and from there listened to Ruth and Chris's voices in the kitchen, above the gush of a kettle being filled and the clatter and tinkle of mugs and teaspoons. I heard the scrape and judder of the back door being opened, and Harry's short triumphant laugh. Then footfalls in the hall, and splashing bathroom noises. I rested my hands on my knees to steady them.

After a minute or two Harry came in, in clean white T-shirt over his jeans, looking fresh and exhilarated. He crossed the room and flung himself into the armchair under the window.

'So,' he said, smiling at me, 'let's have it, then. What'd Maskin been up to?'

The question roused me to fury.

'More to the point,' I said, my voice thick, 'is what the hell *you* were up to. Playing your bloody stupid games. Jesus Christ. You didn't know he'd been up to anything.'

Harry's eyebrows lifted in mild outrage.

'Came back, didn't he? I warned him. I told him what to expect if I saw him again. Fucking creep. Lucky to get off so lightly.'

'Lucky?' I hissed. 'You call that lucky?'

'Yeah, I do. Shit, I didn't touch him.' He spoke with exasperated patience, as if I was being quite ridiculous, but he could see that I wasn't myself (for some reason) so he was making allowances. A thought made him smile; he tried to repress it, failed, and shook his head in amusement. 'Hey, though,' he said, 'he could move, couldn't he?' He gave a delighted laugh.

I sagged back against the sofa. He suddenly seemed a stranger, and an awful grief cut into me. I put a hand to my forehead.

Voices emerged into the hall, ordinary, cheerful voices. They seemed to belong to strangers too. Through my fingers I saw Chris enter the room, then Ruth, both bearing mugs. Chris was grinning at something Ruth had said.

'Jane?' His smile disappeared. 'Hey, Jane, are you all right?'

He moved swiftly towards me. I removed the hand from my forehead, nodded, and gave him a weak smile. He looked relieved – he must have thought I was crying.

'Give her some tea,' said Ruth. Chris thrust a mug into my hand. He put his own on the coffee table, and sat down on the sofa beside me.

'She's OK,' said Harry dismissively, taking his mug from Ruth. 'Just feeling sorry for Maskin.'

'I'm not.' I leant forward savagely. 'Just because I'm angry with you doesn't mean I'm sorry for him.' I turned to Ruth, who had settled herself in the armchair opposite. 'D'you know what he did? Has Chris told you what he did?'

'Yes. He told me.' There was reproach in her voice, but not outrage. Her eyes and mouth still bore traces of the joke she had shared with Chris.

'I don't know how anyone could behave like that. I can't understand it.' I shook my head repeatedly. For a moment I was genuinely near to tears.

'You called the police,' Harry said. 'You wanted them to deal with him.' He shrugged. 'Where's the difference?'

'But you didn't know I'd called them!' I screeched. 'You didn't know what he'd done.'

'OK,' he said tolerantly. 'So what had he done?'

'It's irrelevant.' I didn't want to tell him; I knew it would be used against me.

'Flapped the letter-box cover,' said Chris unthinkingly.

Harry rolled his face upwards and snorted at the ceiling.

'Very frighteningly,' I said hotly. 'And for ages. And he pushed his face into the glass.' I shuddered. 'It was horrible, all squashed and distorted. He wouldn't go away. He stood outside the door begging in this terrible whining voice. You could tell he was doing it to frighten us.' I appealed to Ruth. 'It really was terrifying.'

'I believe you,' she said. All humour had gone from her face.

'There you are, then,' said Harry complacently.

'But it isn't,' I wailed. 'It isn't at all. He's seen the bike now. He'll know it was us. He'll be sure we know where she is. And then you have to do that . . . he's going to be so angry . . . Oh God . . .' I covered my mouth with my hand; I hadn't thought any of this, coherently, till now. The swell of fear almost choked me.

'Hey,' said Chris. He slipped an arm around my shoulders and squeezed them.

For a moment nobody said anything. Ruth stared at Harry. This is your fault, her eyes said; you deal with it. Chris's hand kneaded my shoulder soothingly.

Harry sighed and pushed himself to the edge of the armchair. He leant forward so our knees nearly touched.

'He'll know it was me,' he said. 'He knew it was us already. You know that. Hey . . .' He pushed at my knee. 'You know that, don't you?'

I nodded mutely.

He went on. 'So now he knows it was me, not you. I told him I'd dealt with everything and you'd been kept out of it. Deliberately kept out of it. That you hadn't seen her, or spoken to her, and didn't know where she was. That I'd done everything.' He gave a grim smile. 'And that if he came near you again I'd see that a lot more than his dignity got damaged.' He shook his head emphatically. 'He won't be back.'

'But how d'you know?' I moaned. My anger had vanished; it had been fear, unacknowledged, all along. 'I don't see how you can possibly tell.'

Harry considered, then glanced at Chris. 'What d'you think, then? Go on, you tell her. D'you think he'll be back?'

Chris's arm around me stiffened. Maybe it was just surprise, at being asked.

'No . . .' There was a grudging note in his voice which he seemed to hear and immediately erased with a man-to-man nod. The arm around me relaxed. 'No,' he said again, much more decisively. 'I don't think he'll be back.'

'I know he shouldn't have done it,' Ruth said cautiously, 'but really, the police wouldn't have done much better. They couldn't have arrested him.'

'I know, I know,' I said.

'Nobody got hurt,' she added, 'and he did frighten you.'

'I know.'

'He won't be back,' said Harry. 'He's not stupid. He knows we mean business.' He caught Chris's eye. 'Right?'

'Right,' agreed Chris, and squeezed my shoulder again.

★

And that's how it went. We talked about it for at least another hour, and I became more and more muddled. I knew I was frightened, because I could feel it, and yet Harry seemed so sure of himself. He kept saying, 'It's OK, he'll never bother you again,' with such assurance (and truth, as it turned out) that at times he almost convinced me. In my most reassured moments I even felt churlish not to be more grateful to him, and perhaps I would have been if I hadn't had to witness him exacting his punishment. The others seemed to trust him: Chris had to wrestle with admiring envy for his theft of the glory, and disapproval at its irresponsibility and aggressiveness, but wouldn't condemn him or disagree with his conclusions. Even Ruth – who of course hadn't seen anything – seemed to adopt a resigned 'well it's done now and it could have turned out worse' attitude.

'Sometimes rough justice works better than threats of official action,' she said at one point. 'They'd be pretty empty anyway, over something like this. And if anyone's going to know that, he is.'

I had to agree. All the same, nothing altered the fact that Maskin was still out there, still in one piece, and still hadn't got what he wanted. Nothing could stop me, in deeply unreassured moments, imagining his feelings as he scuttled back to wherever he hid out, and knowing that if I were he, the primary emotion left once I'd got over my fear and humiliation would undoubtedly be fury. And because I'd never seen Maskin angry I probably visualized the result as much more terrifying and uncontrolled than anything in real life could be. I could almost see that suit splitting down the back as the monster within swelled with rage, the veneer of respectability and restraint tossed aside as he exploded into the world in his true malevolent colours. In those moments I knew – though a moment ago I had listened to the others,

and been convinced by them – that I was right, and they
wrong.

Later, I made sense of it. I realized that I was confusing
abstract, rational fear – fear of Maskin, and his fury – with
irrational, personal fear; fear, that is, for my own safety. But
at the time the two seemed inextricable: there didn't seem
anyone but me to be fearful for. It seemed obvious Maskin
was no match for Harry, who was the only other person he
might feel tempted to vent his fury on. And I don't think it
occurred to any of us that in his forceful attempts to divert
Maskin from me Harry had completely disregarded his own
position. That he had gone out of his way, with the things he
had said, and the manner in which he had said them, to draw
Maskin's fire towards himself. It became clear, for instance,
that he had left Maskin with the impression that whilst I
might not know where Joanna was, he certainly did; this was
untrue, of course, but it was typical of Harry that he hadn't
felt inclined to make this point, and had possibly even
enjoyed giving Maskin something else to feel outsmarted
over.

It was all very foolish and dangerous, but he hadn't done it
for himself. He'd done it for me, and as far as I was concerned
it worked, so in a way he was right after all; and I have to
add, too, because these things are never as tidy or obliging as
our principles would have us believe, that if he hadn't done it,
and had tried to deal with Maskin reasonably and not aggressively, someone might still have been hurt, because I don't
think Maskin would have given up. And in that case, without
Harry's foolhardy but ultimately protective tactics, it's
always possible that that someone might have been me.

The evening broke up early. The others would have extended
it into a more sociable gathering, but I was too tired.

Before we left I arranged to meet Harry and Ruth the next day after work for an early evening drink. Chris was taking his daughters to the cinema; I could have gone with him but the thought of suffocating in a cinema in that heat didn't appeal, and a drink outside with friends seemed infinitely preferable to the alternative of an evening alone in the flat.

We settled on the Freemasons' Arms in Hampstead, because of its beer garden, and then Chris and I went upstairs. I spent the rest of the evening trying to convince myself that it really was all over; and this time, in the darkness of bed, it was Chris's turn to do the holding and soothing into unconsciousness.

## Chapter 15

In the morning I woke with my face towards the light. Outside, visible through the undrawn bedroom curtains, a ghostly sun was burning away the dawn haze, rising into a white-blue sky. As I watched my mood stirred and lifted.

At breakfast, I remember, Chris said cautiously, 'You were in a state last night. You OK for work?'

I smiled, recalling as if from a dream myself of twelve hours ago, and said, 'Of course.'

On the journey to work I felt tired, but, once there, forgot about it. The great blessing of work is that there's so much to do, and most of it's dealing with other people. There's no time for yourself. At lunchtime everything tasted of cardboard, but I'd experienced that before after troubled nights and just wondered why I'd wasted my money when I hadn't felt hungry in the first place.

I had two student sessions after lunch and then an hour in the staff room marking and chatting with colleagues until Chris was free. He drove me to Hampstead and dropped me off outside the Freemasons' Arms on his way up to Highgate to pick up his daughters.

The pub was already open but it was only half past five, and the fields of Hampstead Heath lay opposite, green and inviting, so I decided to take a stroll there before the others arrived. I crossed the road and followed a sandy path into tussocky, unmown meadow. In the distance lay the

Hampstead ponds; aimlessly, but drawn to their glassy, liquid beauty, I ambled down to them.

The day was still hot and slow. I stood on the path and gazed out over the brilliant water, at the fine town-house vista beyond, golden-glassed in the late afternoon sun, and then upwards, to the rich cobalt sky. Playground shrieks of splashing children filled my ears. The exoticism of the view lifted my thoughts, detaching them from the present, and pushing them ahead. Soon, I knew, I would have to decide what I was going to do in the holidays. Only a couple of weeks away now; but then I was never one for planning far ahead. When Chris and I had been to Greece the previous summer our choice was influenced more by what cheap tickets were left than anything else. If you don't regard your partner as permanent, it's tempting fate to book a summer holiday together just after Christmas.

As I wandered along beside the water I tried to focus my mind on these prosaic matters, but failed to come to grips with anything so practical and found myself drifting into a wider and more reflective state. The cries of the children faded and seemed to be coming from somewhere else, miles away. My mind wanted to reassess everything, to step back and take the grand view, weigh up the past and contemplate the future; and as I let it, and tasted its conclusions, I was suffused with a sense of regret, a sense that I was allowing my life to slip away without direction, or purpose. It was also a sense of isolation and discontinuity, of me as a speck trudging through life, an emptiness behind me, with both my parents dead, and a void in front, which I had chosen not to fill.

I knew that this sensation, a not unfamiliar one, had been aroused because I was suffering from a reaction to the night before, and perhaps too because of the time of year it was, when one academic year was ending, and a new one, just like the last and even more routine, loomed ahead. I found myself wondering, as I had wondered before, whether it was time to make changes in my life, to do something more challenging with it; but couldn't think of anything that would be more than change for the sake of change, because the really big decisions that might have profoundly redirected my life, such as getting married, or having children, had already been taken irrevocably, years before.

I sat down on the grass and thought about these things for a while, or rather I let these things wash through me and looked on, interested but not deeply involved; we all have moments when we ponder what we are doing, and what it's all about and, although the process is slightly painful, it isn't excessively so, because of the knowledge that it doesn't last. That when real life impinges again the thoughts get relegated to the back of the mind, and forgotten about till next time. It must be part of the human condition to review and be vaguely dissatisfied. Life plods on and moments of joy can't be held for long, even if moments of unhappiness seem to have learnt the secret. So there's always a sense of loss in reflection, and it must be that which makes it nostalgic and painful.

But dreaming by the ponds I didn't mind. I thought of it almost as an indulgence: in the normal course of events my life was placid and anxiety-free, and doubtless it exercised the emotions to use them now and again. That made me sigh then, and think of Berry. Since having the children she'd found it increasingly difficult to listen to classical music, which she loved but found deeply moving and emotional. She said it was because she had quite enough intense feeling in real life now, and had no desire to induce more through music.

I thought, there by the ponds, that she was right: music was a way of stirring the emotions for the sake of it, and in that sense an indulgence, a substitute for the real thing. People claim with something like pride that they can be moved to tears by certain passages; when you can be moved to tears by life itself, it's understandable that your desire for that kind of pointless sensualism should cease.

Because of my ruminations I slightly lost track of time, and it was a quarter past six before I left the Heath and crossed the road again. As I approached the pub I could see over the wall into the garden, and glimpsed Ruth already there, reading a book, with her drink on the trestle table in front of her.

I entered the building, bought myself a lager in the beamed public bar, and stepped outside with it. Seeing her in the distance I thought how attractive she looked, unruffled and coolly smart, even after a day's work in such temperatures. I had been mentally so far away on my stroll that I was still having to make an effort to reconnect myself with the world; looking at her before she saw me I felt that for once I was seeing her as a stranger might, as a woman in her thirties sitting alone. And being aware that a stranger wouldn't know that she was waiting for her friends and lover, I felt a surge of tenderness for her, somehow enhanced by the fact that she didn't look ill at ease sitting alone, as if she were used to it, or had had to get used to it. I wondered if I sometimes inspired the same reaction in others, and amused myself with the thought that tender vibrations might have been wafting my way for years, and I'd never had so much as an inkling of them.

Then she looked up and saw me, and the spell was broken.

'Sorry,' I said, and pulled up a chair beside her. 'I went for a walk.'

'It's OK,' she said. She tucked a marker into her paperback and blinked and stretched her eyes. It looked as if she might have been some way away too.

We sat and chatted and watched the other people there, and thought aloud about pub food, because Chris wouldn't be back to collect me until after nine, and we'd be incapable if we didn't fill up with something before then.

Half-past six came and went, and then seven. Ruth began to look at her watch and wonder where Harry was.

'What time did he say he'd come?' I asked.

'Half-six.' She ticked impatiently. 'I bet he's fallen asleep. I'll give him a ring.'

She went inside to use the telephone. A minute later she returned, saying there was no reply.

'He must be on his way,' I said.

'Yes,' she agreed.

But another quarter of an hour passed, and we both knew it was only ten minutes on a motorbike from Kilburn to Hampstead.

Ruth rang him again: there was still no reply. She began to get anxious and cross with him, as one does in the first mild stages of panic.

I said, 'He's stopped off somewhere, I bet.' But a creeping coldness was wrapping itself around me, too.

By half-seven Ruth's eyes were locked on to the open bar doors.

'Where the hell is he?' she said tightly, after a crowd of young men had spilt out into the garden, none of them Harry. 'Christ, he can't have forgotten.'

I didn't ask what she thought might have happened; I was too frightened myself now, and I didn't want to say what my fears were. I didn't even want to say them to myself.

We tried to distract ourselves with other topics of conversation, but it didn't work. Ruth became more and more restless.

At eight she cracked the mood wide open by standing up and saying she was going home.

I stood up too and said quietly, 'I'll come with you.'

We went inside to ring for a taxi, which arrived within two minutes. And then we left.

I can hardly remember the journey home. In what we were doing we had both admitted our fear, and it didn't need spelling out more than that. I don't think anything much was said at all. Ruth sat on the very edge of her seat, urging the taxi on with her tension, and as we drew near my sight seemed to improve, and my hearing fade, because you always imagine the worst, and this time it was unimaginable.

I don't know how to go on without shocking. I can't get round it.

But then, I suddenly realized, that is exactly as it should be. Exactly as it was.

We found Harry on the bathroom floor. Semi-conscious, drenched, and doll-like with exhaustion. His hands were tied behind his back with flex from the hall table lamp, and he had been beaten and half drowned under the mixer tap of the bath. In his struggles he had hit his head repeatedly on the metal jutting out above him, and the bath itself was gruesome: blood and hair everywhere.

Just outside, on the hall carpet, among shards of mirror and broken pieces of lamp, were two billiard cues, one whole, one snapped off near the tip.

Ruth cut him free and held him till the ambulance arrived. Perhaps she shouldn't have, because of his injuries, but I'm glad she did; I think he knew who it was, and would have wanted it.

She went with him in the ambulance, while I stayed in the flat with the police. So at least she was with him at the end; he died before they reached the hospital. One of the policemen left the ruined hall to answer the phone, and when he returned he said, 'He didn't make it,' to his mates, and they looked at each other, and then at me. The policeman glanced round apologetically, almost shyly, and I managed to say, 'It's all right, I'm only a neighbour,' and he looked relieved.

I don't know why I said that, why I still felt compelled to consider someone else's feelings. It must be ingrained very deep.

I couldn't cry, not then. There was too much horror. I suddenly felt suffocated by the mess, and the men sifting through the mess, and their voices as they worked, and I stumbled into the kitchen to get air. The back door was ajar and I didn't care about fingerprints or disturbing evidence or anything. I was just bursting with something and had to get out.

And then I saw his bike. That's when the tears came, and once they'd come they were unstoppable.

It lay in pieces on the concrete around me: there was battered metal, and buckled chrome, and broken glass, and dripping oil, and the stench of petrol, but, really, no bike any more. The caretaker's sledgehammer from the boiler house lay amongst it, the cast-iron head wedged in the twisted wreckage of the frame.

I prayed Harry hadn't had to watch, but knew he had, and couldn't cope with the thought. I must have made a noise, because a policeman came out and asked me if I was all right.

I batted at the air between us and gasped, 'Leave me alone, please.'

He stared around and muttered, 'Christ. Bastards.' And went back in again.

I sat on the fire escape steps with my head in my hands, and tried to think who Maskin could have got to help him, because I knew he couldn't have done this on his own. And why in God's name anyone should have wanted to help him, and hurt

Harry. I pleaded with someone to tell me Harry had felt only anger when he had watched them doing this to the bike. And he couldn't have known he was going to die; so he might not have been too afraid.

But nothing I told myself helped. I needed unconsciousness: the pictures crowding into my mind were too agonizing to bear. Especially the quiet ones: Harry kneeling on the floor upstairs, concentrated, skilful, happy; Harry drunk and charming, damp and longing, kissing me; and Harry with Jamie and Zoe, natural and tolerant, relaxed in the company of children he was never going to have; everything was unthinkable, and I couldn't stop the tears.

Then rage stirred, and forced connections. I tried to fill my mind with other things, to smother the thought of Harry in the hands of those who meant him harm, but it all joined itself up and led me home to him. I thought of the kids who broke into my flat, teenage vandals on their way to the big time; I thought of the boys at the bus stop and their mindless fury, and the policemen who had used their handcuffs; I thought of football fans rampaging on the High Street, and others rioting on the stands. I thought of Chris, maiming that girl because of his stupidity and aggression, and drunken Irishmen crashing chairs down on their friends. I thought of Brian, jealous and hostile, eager to do down; and I even thought of Jamie, innocent little Jamie, fighting under the games table, beating the fruit trees, and duelling with his peace dove.

My mind opened up to let the others flood in. I was overwhelmed by Tamils and Singhalese, Sikhs and Hindus, IRA men and Lebanese, Americans and Soviets, murderers and maniacs and brawlers and wife-beaters, and suddenly all the images rushed together, and all the men in the world were at war. Maskin and a faceless shadow beside him peered through the shell-fire, foot-soldiers with only billiard cues and fists, instead of bombs and guns, but still under orders, and part of the action.

And then I thought again of Harry, poor dear foolish difficult Harry, tortured and dead, and as I sat there staring at what had once been his life, twisted and glinting and scattered across the concrete, it all roared up into a maelstrom of pain and violence, and at that moment I hated every one of them.

# Epilogue

Harry's life cost seven pints of beer at lunchtime, and the promise of the same again when the job was done. They said they hadn't meant to kill him.

The other man's name was Hill – most appropriate for someone so large and bovine and peasantlike – and he had never met Maskin before that day. But he had listened to him in the pub as he drank the beer bought for him, and been indignant that Maskin's life had been threatened and his wife spirited away by some young motorbike thug. Maskin had picked his man well; Hill appeared to regard his participation as a positive duty of outraged friendship.

They said that if Harry had been more co-operative and had shown more contrition he wouldn't have got so hurt; and who knows, that may well be true. Poor Harry, he can't have wanted to go out like that, whatever Ruth says. I can understand her bitterness, but I'm sure he couldn't help himself. He'd had a lot of disappointments in life he could do nothing about, and to object strenuously to further threat must have seemed all he had left. He had to show that, whatever he was forced to accept, he couldn't be defeated. Winners and losers again, the same old story.

And in any case, even if he had been more willing to accept defeat, he still couldn't tell Maskin what he wanted to know, and they didn't believe him when he finally did tell them that. They had broken up the bike to encourage him, and he had already been hurt by then, but not fatally, and then Hill had rewarded himself with whisky he found in the kitchen, and Maskin alone had bent Harry over the bath. It wasn't his fault, he said, that Harry had killed himself by cutting his head open on the tap.

My anger has faded, slowly. You can't keep rage up for ever, and it is very weakening when there is nowhere to put it. It was intense at the funeral, though, which was a terrible ordeal because nearly everybody had come for Ruth and not for Harry. His father was there, still wrestling with brave faces, and the Director of the Assessment Centre, and two young men from Brighton came up just for him, but everybody else was Ruth's, and she was so grateful to the two young men that she embarrassed them, and they didn't stay long.

And since most people were sorry for Ruth, rather than angry for Harry, all the words were about healing, and reconciliation, and coming to terms, and I wanted to howl, because I didn't want to come to terms with anything. In my anger I felt, and still feel, though the passion has dimmed, that we had all done enough coming to terms with monstrous things like this, and that it was no longer enough to regret and deplore, and fail to make the connections. We all have to die but nobody should have to die as Harry did, and nobody should have to grieve and remember how he died as Ruth has to. I looked at the faces around me, full of shocked sympathy and grim resignation but nothing else, and frightened myself with my rage. I felt the world didn't care – not just about Harry, although it didn't care much about him – but about anybody. Because if it did, I thought, if people just looked at what was happening and truly cared, really let it touch them, they'd do something about it.

*

After the funeral I went to Norwich and spent the summer holiday with Berry and Brian. Of course we didn't tell Jamie and Zoe what had actually happened. They believed violence was like it was on the television, and we must protect the children. I came back for a few weekends to see Ruth; she was staying with her brother in Putney and coping frighteningly well – emotionally on hold, I thought. I didn't see anything of Chris because I was feeling so angry and fragile and didn't want to sleep with anyone, and I knew he would want to.

When the case came to court the prosecution were only interested in proving their case, and not in protecting Harry's name; I didn't recognize him as the man I knew from what was said about him. Perhaps he wouldn't have minded, but I did, and so did Ruth. What he had done may have been unwise, and even provocative, but he had done it for other people, not himself, and it was his life that was lost, rather than perhaps Joanna's, or even mine, and that point was never made.

The defence was allowed to get away with describing him as a violent bully, as someone who had continually threatened Maskin, interfered wilfully in his marital affairs, and whom Maskin had good reason to believe had deliberately manipulated the affections of his ex-wife.

The prosecution had no interest in disputing these claims, or at least re-interpreting them, because they were irrelevant to the plain facts of the murder. They were only concerned to establish that Maskin and his accomplice intended to do Harry harm, for whatever reason, and might have known that what they were doing was likely to lead to his death.

The newspapers weren't very interested, either. The local papers followed the case but saw it as little more than a drunken brawl between violently inclined men over a domestic and therefore unimportant issue, and regarded the victim, being a young single male adult, unemployed and a biker, as unworthy of any particular outrage or sympathy. They might as well have said: nothing to get excited about, it was just men fighting.

Maskin and Hill were found not guilty of murder, but guilty· of manslaughter. The judge accepted a degree of provocation but professed himself appalled by the brutality of the assault. All the same, his head was screwed on only marginally straighter than the jury's: he gave Maskin four years and Hill two, and when I realized that even without parole Maskin would serve less than three years, and Hill just sixteen months or so, assuming they behaved like good little boys in prison, and that because of them Harry was dead and Ruth bereft, it made me want to spit.

After the court case I didn't see Ruth for a while because she went down to her parents' place in Chichester. Everything suddenly caved in on her, and her work were understanding and gave her leave of absence until she felt better.

She wrote to me, though, and I wrote back, and she said she wanted to see me when she returned, which surprised me because I felt so responsible for the whole thing. I knew I wasn't really to blame, any more than Brian was, but she must still have been aware, as I was, that if she and Harry hadn't moved in below me, and I had never met them and become their friend, none of this would have happened.

In our letters we wrote about Harry, and she said it was a comfort. Her parents hadn't liked him much because he wasn't good enough for her, and although her brother had liked him and was sympathetic she found it difficult to talk about Harry without crying, which he couldn't take. I hope I was some use to her, as I know she was to me. I still saw Chris at work, but my grief was unforgiving and walled him out. So I needed someone to share it with too.

Ruth and Harry's flat was re-let to an old couple who were quite excited about the idea of living in a place where a murder had been committed, and they got on with the Rosens like a house on fire. Mrs Rosen said it would never have happened if the other flats hadn't been empty, because someone would have heard something, so really it was the landlord's fault.

I took nearly two years to move from the flats. I couldn't bring myself to turn my back and desert the ghosts. But after Ruth returned it was awkward because I couldn't ask her to visit, and eventually I realized I was being maudlin and self-indulgent. It was Ruth Harry loved, after all, not me.

I live in Battersea now.